Castlecottage

Copyright Amanda Lee Keller © 2023. All rights reserved.

No part of this book may be used or reproduced by any means, graphic, electronic, or mechanical, including photocopying, recording, taping or by any information storage retrieval system without the written permission of the publisher.

Published by Mater Media
St. Louis, Missouri
www.matermedia.org

Editor: Kari Sherman and Audra Breer
Cover Concept: Cannan Keller
Cover Design and Interior Composition: Trese Gloriod

979-8-9887392-0-3

CASTLECOTTAGE

Amanda Lee Keller

MATER
MEDIA

Dedicated to
Our Lady of Sorrows

CHAPTER 1

shellakiepookie

Josephine catches a glimpse of herself in the gilded antique mirror as she shuffles down the hall. She pauses for a moment to drink in her reflection and marvel at the passing of time.

Her sagging cheeks and craggy nose are in sharp contrast to the youthful glow exuding from the old photo hanging beside her. As she glances to the right, the two young girls in the colorless print stare back with cheeky grins.

"Ah, Maeve, I'll be seein' ye soon," she whispers as she turns from the collection of family photos and continues her painful quest towards the kitchen.

A cardinal blush saturates the room as Josephine hobbles toward the window. With her wrinkled hand, she pulls the slightly yellowed lace curtains to one side, letting the light greet the creases of her face. She squints her pale blue eyes, scanning her dominion.

The venerable stone bridge in front of her cottage stands at attention, straddling the rushing waters of the River Suir.

Black and white dairy cows graze in the lush grassy field while the overcast sky fills the space between Earth and Heaven. In the distance, the grand mountain Slievenamon stares back at Josephine, one old woman to another. The scene shimmers with splendid enchantment.

Suddenly, the pastoral serenity is pierced by a loud shriek and a dark shadow overhead. Josephine reflexively ducks and raises her arm even though she's protected by the sturdy walls of the cottage. A great white owl swoops down, claiming ownership of the garden wall.

The bird perches regally, slowly swiveling its head to lock its marble gaze on Josephine. Its enchanting, golden eyes appear to hold a heavenly prophecy.

"Ah, are ye finishing the hunt? I'm close behind ye, as ye know." Many people would be perturbed at the news of their impending death, but not Josephine. She has lived an honest and full life, and is prepared for her next chapter. Josephine lets the lace fall back over the window and heads to the stove to prepare a curative tea.

Shortly after the kettle begins to whistle, she spies the owl soaring off to roost in the crumbling castle keep attached to the corner of her meager cottage home. "I wonder if ye will miss me," she muses aloud, as if the creature could hear or understand her.

Josephine pours boiling water over a handful of fresh herbs and sets the kettle back on the stove.

The steeping complete, she carries her porcelain cup to her spindle chair and carefully lowers herself into it. The slight squeak of the wood is her faithful companion as her weight fills the seat.

While she sips the steaming liquid, she hears scurrying across the pebbles of the back entrance, followed by a rap on the door.

"Come in!"

The heavy door swings open, and a young, haggard woman with a squirming baby in her arms steps inside. The baby wheezes with a deep croupy cough.

"Josephine, can ye help me?" The woman gasps as she sweeps her dark, wind-tousled hair out of her eyes. "My baby has the whoopin' cough, and none of the medicine the doctor gave is workin'. I'm growin' frantic."

Josephine, getting up as quickly as her worn body will allow, beckons the young woman to come near. "I'll fix the wee one, Freda. There's one more healin' within me yet, God-willin'. Have a seat by the hearth."

The woman takes the hacking child over to the fireplace and sits on one of the rustic wooden stools.

Josephine sets her tea on a pedestal end table and shuffles to a large hutch in the far corner of the room. She opens the creaky pine doors, revealing a collection of unlabeled glass jars. They stand like soldiers, housing an array of herbs, flowers, liquids, and shriveled bits of this and that. Josephine grabs the remedy from a middle shelf.

"Take the blanket from the babe."

Freda unfurls the crocheted quilt as instructed, causing both the crying and coughing to intensify.

Josephine brings over a jar of small brown nuggets and reaches out to the child's forehead. Upon her touch, the infant begins to calm, its wailing and barking replaced by a steady, rumbling wheeze. Josephine closes her eyes, makes the Sign of the Cross on herself, then places her hand once more on the baby's head while mumbling in old Irish.

She carefully unscrews the lid of the jar and extracts one of the pellets, placing it inside the child's mouth. "Hold her mouth till she's swallowed it good."

"What 'tis it?"

"Ferret's-leavins."

"No, dear God!" Freda gasps as she makes a frenzied move to try to remove the morsel.

Josephine firmly grabs Freda's wrist to stop her. "Leave it be. The cough will stop with the final swallow."

Freda relents and scrunches her face in disgust as the baby moves the contents around in her mouth. As the women wait, the child begins to quiet, her breathing returning to a normal rhythm shortly after the contents have slipped down her throat.

Freda puts her ear to her daughter's chest and listens for a few moments before drawing her hand to her mouth in amazement. "The cough is gone, it is!"

"Of course, 'tis gone," Josephine says. "But that wart on yer hand isn't."

Freda glances at the bump on her thumb and quickly tucks her hand under the baby's blanket. "Oh, 'tis nothing."

Josephine returns the jar of ferret droppings to its spot on the crowded shelf while Freda wraps the baby and begins to stand.

Josephine returns with two new jars. "Sit down and show me the wart, girl."

Freda reluctantly returns to the stool and holds her hand out to the old woman.

Josephine reaches two wrinkled, blotchy fingers into one of the jars, plucking out a live snail. It wiggles in her grasp.

Freda's eyes grow wide as she examines the slimy shelled creature. "Wh- What are ye goin' to do with that?" She swallows hard.

"I'll take the shellakiepookie here and place it on yer wart."

Freda nervously looks towards the door.

"Oh, c'mon now. Ye make the Sign of the Cross."

Freda takes a deep breath and crosses herself, clutching her baby tighter to her chest. She returns her hand to Josephine, biting her lip.

"With Mother Mary's blessin', yer hands will be scourged no more." Josephine rubs the snail up and down on the wart three times. With the final pass, she removes a twiggy thorn from the second jar.

Freda quickly retracts her hand from the old woman's reach, "Ye'll not stick me!"

"I'll be needin' your hand and the snail back, dearie."

Freda cautiously returns her hand. Josephine impales the snail with the sharp thorn.

As the snail withers, so does the wart.

Freda's emerald eyes widen in awe. "Yer a miracle worker, Josephine."

Josephine wags her finger. "None of that talk. My gift is from God, no power comes from me."

From the corner of her eye, Josephine spies a snail slithering up to the mouth of the open jar. She gently flicks it to the bottom, replacing the lid before it has a chance to escape.

While rocking the babe in her arms, Freda says, "What would we do without ye, Josephine?

"Ah, you'll learn. Now ye get yerself to Confession so the heal sticks. If ye aren't well in the soul, yer body stands no chance of holding health either," Josephine instructs as she gently ushers mother and child to the back door.

Freda shakes her head from side to side and clutches the St. Benedict medal hanging from the gold chain around her neck. "I heard what happened to Ronan last week."

"Well, what did he expect? Of course his rash came back!" Josephine scoffs. "Physical ailments are often a reflection of the soul. The healin' won't last unless ye get yerself to Confession. He should've known better than to skip the most important part."

Freda nods in agreement. "I'll go first thing in the mornin' when Father Adrian is in. What is it I owe? I'll bring it by after Confession."

"No need. I'll not be here tomorrow. Confession is all you owe."

"A day trip, yer takin? It's been a while since folk have seen ye elsewhere than church."

Josephine carefully crafts her response, recalling the owl's ominous warning.

"I'll be gone fer a *bit* longer than that. It's a trip *well* overdue."

"Godspeed, Josephine."

"Take care of that little one. She's a beauty, that she is."

Josephine escorts mother and child to the door and watches them proceed up the rocky path toward town before retreating inside the cottage.

Once the pair is out of sight, she reaches for the lone wool coat hanging amid a line of empty hooks. She forces her aching arms into the sleeves. Her bony fingers slowly guide each button through its hole. Smoothing her silver-pearl hair, she dons her signature floppy, sky-colored hat.

A rosary of the same shade of blue dangles from a single nail in the crimson wall. She slips the sacred string from its rusted post and runs her fingers over the crucifix.

"I best be to church 'fore it's too late," she whispers as she tucks the rosary in her pocket.

Josephine crosses the threshold, letting the old Alder wood door slam behind her.

CHAPTER 2

The Confession

Josephine sits alone in the back pew of the little chapel at the friary, rubbing her aching knees with her fingers clasped around her beads. Stained glass and the aroma of incense surround her. She recalls an old Irish proverb—*Don't fear an ill wind if your haystacks are tied down*—and decides she best not delay in getting herself some rope.

Gingerly, Josephine hoists herself to her feet and slowly makes her way down the carpeted aisle. At the front of the church, a Franciscan friar is kneeling at the altar rail in prayer. She reaches out and taps him on the shoulder with her bony finger.

"Ahhhh!" The man practically leaps from the kneeler, eyes bulging.

"Father Adrian, I'm sorry. I didn't mean to startle ye."

"Josephine!" He gawps at the elderly woman and sighs. "I thought all had left after Mass." He looks over his shoulder and examines the rest of the chapel to make sure there aren't any other surprises.

Rather than explain to a man more than thirty years her junior that her stealth is the result of the slow and painful movements of old age, she continues to the business at hand.

"Will ye hear a confession now, Father?"

"Now?" Father Adrian purses his lips, balking at the suggestion that he stray from the weekly schedule. "You know, confessions are *tomorrow*."

Josephine keeps her eye contact and crosses her arms. The uncooperative friar reads the look of determination on her face.

"I suppose I can hear it today."

"Good." Josephine looks at him expectantly, hoping the ill wind won't strike before she has the chance to cleanse her soul.

Father Adrian takes a deep breath, and exhales with a note of exasperation "Well...just give me a moment. I'll meet ye in the confessional."

The priest abruptly stands and turns his back on her with a distinct air of impatience, then stops to tend to a candle on the altar.

Josephine rolls her eyes at his back before sharing a look with Christ on the Cross. She whispers to Jesus, "That's Yer shepherd."

Josephine enters the dimly lit confessional and lowers herself into the wooden chair. She runs her withered hands down her thighs to smooth her dress. After placing her hat in her lap, she drapes her rosary over her right hand and presses her palms together, quietly preparing to share her transgression.

The little door slides open, revealing the friar's silhouette through the blackened screen.

Josephine starts the ritual with the Sign of the Cross. "Bless me Father, fer I have sinned. Tis been six days since my last confession."

"What is it ye wish to confess?"

"Father, I have done nothin' of grave sin since my last confession."

The friar exhales loudly and scratches his chin. "Then why have ye insisted on confession *today*?"

Josephine clutches the beads in her hand a bit tighter. "Father, the sin I wish to confess happened many years ago, and until the act was recounted in my dream last night, I'd never felt the need to mention it. Upon closer reflection, now I do, and I must confess and repent."

The priest drops his shoulders and sighs. "Yes, go on."

Josephine readjusts in the chair, causing it to let out a small squeak. "I score it as some 54 years ago, after the birth of my twins. My mother, God rest her soul, insisted she would watch the babies while Teddy, God rest his soul, and I went out on the town. We'd not gone out since our wedding. It goes without sayin', I was desperate for craic." Josephine pauses briefly, waiting for an empathetic gesture.

"Understandable. Go on."

"Well, we'd a few pints and many a laugh. Oh, we were havin' a brilliant time. Everyone in town must have squeezed into the pub that night. I don't think I'd ever seen it so crammed."

Father Adrian lifts his wrist to check his watch. "Yes, Josephine, and yer sin?"

"Oh, yes, well…Teddy got up to go to the loo just as a sing-song broke out. Next thing I knew, that rascal Denis McClure, God rest his soul, grabbed me and pulled me to the dance floor. His wife, my dear friend, ye know, Immaculata, well, she was to Cork visiting her mother, leavin' Denis a bachelor for the night."

Josephine closes her eyes, transporting herself back in time. For a moment, the pain seems to leave her crippled limbs as the scene in her mind takes shape.

"We whirled and whirled, oh I was dizzy with dance, good craic fer sure. When the song ended, Denis sat down with me in the snug. Teddy was still not back from the loo, probably talkin' to the many heads along the way." Josephine smiles at the thought of her jovial, late husband. "Denis and I began re-hashin' our school days. What a cheeky bunch we were with the nuns. It's a wonder we weren't thrashed to bits. The recollections went on and on until, well, I'm sure it was the pints talking..."

Another Irish proverb pops into Josephine's head. *Don't tell your secret, even to a fence.* She decides to lower her voice a bit before continuing.

"Ye see, Father, Denis began fessing how he always fancied me growing up, but that Teddy nabbed me first. Not a word could I respond before that divil, Denis, kissed me!...and...I kissed him back. Thank God we were in the snug out of eye-shot. Teddy never knew. Sweet Jesus, forgive me." Josephine moves her hand to her chest and shakes her head in shame.

The friar contains a smile, tickled that this white-haired, hat-wearing, snaggle-toothed, woman was confessing her amorous indiscretions now, after 54 years. "Was that the only time this happened?"

"Oh yes, Father, the one and only time."

"Probably best ye didn't mention to yer husband since ye had no feelings for Denis."

Josephine nods in agreement, "Yes, like I said, the pints."

A chuckle nearly escapes from the priest. "The pints."

Father Adrian regains his somber tone. "And yer thoughts were devoted to yer husband from then on?"

"Teddy was my only love, to be sure, Father. There was of course an occasional movie star type I'd fancy, but that was all in good fun, not nearly a sin would ye say, Father?"

"Fancying movie stars is usually given a pass. Have ye any other confessions?"

"No, Father."

"Josephine, your penance is to say one *Hail Mary* for every year you failed to confess this sin. Now make an Act of Contrition."

After Josephine mumbles the prayer, Father Adrian says the sacred words of absolution and concludes with, "Go and sin no more."

"Thank ye, Father."

Josephine stands a little easier with this weight off her shoulders and returns her trademark hat to her head. When she begins to leave the confessional, Father Adrian stops her.

"Josephine, one more thing."

She pauses, and in the momentary silence she can hear the priest tapping his foot on the floor.

"Ye waited 54 years... why exactly couldn't this have waited for the scheduled confession time *tomorrow*?"

Josephine pauses to ponder for a moment before deciding to keep the omen of the owl's dayside visit to herself. "Well, Father...the morrow will not be mine. This moment is. A clean soul is all I need to complete God's mission on earth."

The friar nods in puzzled agreement as Josephine departs to go complete her penance.

While she is praying at the altar rail, a man dressed in farm-hand attire bursts into the chapel and plops into a kneel. He scoots in a most reverent manner toward Josephine, taking his place next to her. Leaning slightly toward her, he whispers, "Josephine."

Josephine opens one eye to squint at who is speaking. She whispers back, "Owen...I'm doing penance, for God's sake, man!"

Father Adrian busies about the altar, overhearing the low commotion.

"I'm sorry Josephine, but folks are searching all over town fer ye. Several pairs of eyes saw you headin' here."

"Ahem." Josephine clears her throat loudly and then cuts her eyes from Owen to the priest and then back. "This is not the place for such discussions."

Josephine closes her eyes and recites her prayer a little louder to make her message clearer. "Hail Mary, full of grace, the Lord is with Thee..."

"Josephine! This is not about needin' a healin'. There's an American lookin for ye. Say yer penance later, woman!"

Josephine's eyes snap open. "American? Lookin' for me? Are ye sure?"

Owen nods excitedly as he tucks his thumbs behind the straps of his denim overalls.

"Oh dear." Josephine clutches her rosary to her chest as she puts two and two together. *Could this be what the owl was hooting about? Did I just confess in haste?"*

Where is the peaceful, solitary passing she had envisioned for today? From the looks of her two visitors, a slow and painful martyr's death seems more likely.

Micheleen turns to Maeve. "Wouldn't you like seeing where Pop-Pop used to live, Maeve? Maeve, stop playing that game, honey, please!"

Maeve momentarily glances up at Josephine before returning her attention to the tablet.

Josephine studies the black-haired moppet sitting in front of her. It seems this child wouldn't muster a kind look toward Josephine to save her wretched little soul.

Josephine decides the girl must be a product of nannies or American day care… and the most dreaded babysitter of all, that mind-numbing screen of distortion. Such a device would sour even the best-tempered child. A look of disgust creeps over Josephine's face as she observes the scowling waif with her silly blue cap.

Micheleen continues to ramble as the waiter delivers a piping hot tray of food. The visitors dig in while Josephine silently bows her head to say grace.

"Wow, this smoked salmon is delicious!" Micheleen wipes her mouth with a napkin, leaving a red smudge from her lipstick.

Josephine carefully scoops a spoonful of shepherd's pie and places the perfectly-crafted mixture of buttery potatoes, seasoned vegetables, and tender ground beef in her mouth. The delectable meal almost makes trying to decipher the annoying American accent bearable.

Josephine takes a sip of water as Micheleen announces, "… So with my divorce final and my new position with the cosmetics company here, the signs became clear. Maeve and I are going to live with you in Castlecottage like Granny and my dad did! We're going to take care of you for the rest of your life, Auntie Jo. Isn't that great?"

The words "for the rest of your life" seemed to escape from Micheleen's lips in slow motion. Josephine, shocked and in mid-swallow, almost chokes, spewing water like a bathing elephant all over the back of a passing waiter.

Amongst the commotion of the soaked man and Josephine's coughing, little Maeve chortles with delight, cracking her stony grimace for the first time and unleashing a thoroughly infectious gap-toothed grin.

"Oh, Auntie Jo, are you alright?" Micheleen says, passing Josephine a pile of napkins.

In between coughing and patting the water from her face, Josephine squeaks out, "Yes. I must've had a tickle in my throat."

Sweet Jesus, help me. Why didn't you just let me choke?

Almost as if someone is playing a cruel prank, in walks Immaculata McClure, the very widow of Denis "the Kisser" McClure himself.

Josephine sighs, remembering her unfinished Hail Marys as Immaculata heads in their direction.

"Josephine Byrne! What brings ye and yer blue hat to town? Someone must have quite an illness for ye to make a house call!"

Josephine reluctantly makes the introductions. "Immaculata, this is Michael's girl, Micheleen, and her little one, Maeve."

Micheleen and Immaculata shake hands. Immaculata smiles as she looks in Maeve's direction.

"Maeve, is it? Named after yer sister? But she's the head of yerself at that age, Jo, not yer sister at all. That dark hair and, oh, those blue eyes, she's ye all over again!"

Little Maeve's smile melts to horror at being likened to such an old, ugly woman. Josephine is equally averse to the comparison.

"No, Immaculata, she favors her American relatives to be sure. Not an Irish feature on her that I can see."

"Ah but she does. Look, the two of ye are twins with yer blue hats on; yer even missing the same teeth!"

The truth of this comparison hits Josephine and Maeve simultaneously as they stare blankly at each other.

Micheleen jumps in. "My gosh, you *are* missing the same teeth! Isn't that cute?"

With Josephine and Maeve still eyeing one another, Immaculata turns to Micheleen, "So you're Michael's girl, are ye?"

Micheleen nods.

"I knew yer dah as a boy. My husband, Denis, and Josephine's husband, Teddy, were fast friends all their lives. Now it's just their two old widows left, ay Jo?"

Josephine nods in glazed agreement, wondering if she has already died and gone to hell.

CHAPTER 4

Scratch of the Owl

After lunch, Josephine reluctantly leads the duo home to Castlecottage.

"*Take care of you*" Micheleen had said. As if Josephine needed anyone to take care of her on her final day; all she needed was some alone time to complete her penance and a silent place to pass in peace. The uninvited visitors were causing her final day to be much longer than she had anticipated.

Micheleen presses on the thick brown Alder door, revealing the unusual shade of blue coating the entry hall. "Wow, this is some shade. It's sapphire, or is it cobalt, Auntie Jo? It seems to change depending on where I'm standing."

"It's blue," Josephine says curtly.

Micheleen nods absentmindedly as she looks down and picks up a letter lying on the floor below the mail slot.

"Ah, here's the letter I sent you. Guess we were meant to surprise you!" Micheleen chuckles as she sets the letter on the entry table.

over 13 years now. Done right, this cloth will stop the bleedin' of any superficial wound."

Micheleen looks at Maeve's head, mystified while Josephine heads to the car as fast as her arthritic state allows.

Maeve rubs where the wound had been. She looks at her blood-free hand before plunking her baseball cap back on without the faintest hint of awe or gratitude.

CHAPTER 5

Last rite, wrong

Micheleen slams on the breaks, bringing the tiny red rental car to an abrupt halt just outside the friary. Josephine winces in pain as she tries to get out, her arthritic joints locking up. Micheleen responds to the groans by rushing to the passenger side to help the elderly bird hatch from her metal shell.

As Josephine begins to stand, her hat grazes the top of the doorframe and pitches over the seat to the back. Neither of the women notice. The blue cotton chapeau lands right at Maeve's feet, breaking her technology trance. She plops her tablet on her lap and picks up the hat, clenching it tightly in her fists, crumpling the hat as the scapegoat for this unwanted move to Ireland.

Micheleen helps Josephine reach a standing, albeit curved, position. "Easy, there ya go. Are you alright?"

Josephine struggles to be grateful for the help. "Yes, I'll be fine. Now off with ye."

Josephine curls her toes and purses her lips. "Is there any other kind?"

"Though I doubt your mortality is coming as soon as ye say, yer death amongst kin would be a comfort, would it not?"

"Argh, comfort? Ye've not heard their accents and all their techno gadgetry. The hounds of hell would howl more sweetly." Josephine flinches. "They're here to prolong my earthly pain, not to aid in its passing. I fear the longer I'm around them, the longer I'm around!"

The friar scratches his head. "Josephine, yer not making sense. What is it really? Are ye fearful they're here for yer land?"

"Heaven's no! Are ye not listening to me, man…I mean, Father? I've had a long life with much grief and joys to be sure, but the truth is, I don't want any more family…all that I had I've lost. What I need is to be with the ones that have passed from me, the sooner the better. I'm too old, and in too much pain, to be accommodatin' strangers. These Americans are trying to turn my life upside down! Help me, Father, I'm desperate. I'm done–"

"Josephine, slow down." Father Adrian interrupts. "God and yer family in Heaven have sent yer visitors here for a divine reason–"

Josephine returns the interruption. "Oh shite! … I mean, please excuse my language, Father. What I mean to say is…. Well, for God's sake, I just want to be alone with my memories. These people stand for all the things I despise: the spread of modern infection, the replacin' of the sacred with the secular, the whims of the individual versus the wants of God. They are no family of mine. I simply want to die in peace. Have I not earned that at my age?"

The priest sucks in a deep breath, exhales, and then pauses for a few moments before speaking slowly. "There's a purpose at work that ye must see through to its end."

Josephine leans a little closer and slows the pace of her speech to enunciate each word. "Father, I am dying today." Her desperation grows as the speed of the words increase. "Ye must administer the Last Rites to me now. God shall grant me death. If not, I will see to it myself…I will!"

Father Adrian gasps, "Yer death is not yers to grant, Josephine Byrne!"

Josephine stares straight ahead at the Cross and thinks about her *real* family – her son and daughter who died in a car crash when they were merely teens, her sister and closest friend who passed more than a decade ago, and Teddy, who left her completely alone, solidifying her recluse status. Tears well in her tired eyes.

The priest's expression softens as he puts a comforting hand on her shoulder. "Josephine, I know ye've had a hard life. Maybe the Lord has more in store for ye in your last days than outings to daily Mass and visits from the town incurables. Maybe ye have other important work to be done?" He glances over to a statue of the Pietà underneath one of the stained-glass windows and then looks at Josephine's withered face. "Ye know…ye have much in common with Our Mother. She, too, suffered immense sorrow in her earthy life and longed to be with her child in Heaven after He was gone."

Father Adrian reaches into his pocket and pulls out a circular silver medal. "I've been carrying this with me for weeks. I think today is the day I shall pass it on."

He gently picks up Josephine's wrinkled hand, presses the

CHAPTER 6

Cold Curse

Micheleen tries to coax Maeve out of the car. "Sweetie, the owl isn't going to hurt you. Pop-Pop always said the old owl protects us from bad things."

Maeve is firmly planted in the back seat with her arms crossed. "It bit me!"

"Oh honey, it did not. Its toenail hit you by mistake."

Micheleen realizes she isn't making much headway with her daughter and exhales loudly in exasperation.

"Okay, I'll go look for the owl and make sure it's sleeping." She shuts the car door and leaves Maeve to sulk with her video game.

Micheleen stands erect and breathes in the crisp Irish breeze. She takes in the picturesque view with a sense of pride. This is the land of her father and the generations before him. This is the spot her father talked about whenever the two of them were alone. It was the part of his heart he could only share with his daughter. The stories were his gift to her, and now, here in this place, they're coming alive, along with his memory.

Micheleen admires the effortless beauty of the cottage home. Wooden boxes grace each window, overflowing with an endless array of flowers. Like an elderly duke ushering the arm of a middle-aged country girl, the moss-laden castle keep is sutured to the quaint cottage structure for all eternity. Though they were erected in different architectural eras, this odd pairing of the castle ruin and the little brown house complement one another. Like most couples in Ireland, they make it work; however, the obvious age difference is beginning to put a strain on the relationship. The simple provincial home labors to steady the once majestic castle keep. Built as the manor home to Lords and Ladies, the genteel edifice of the keep is now worn down, its tumbling stone form able to house only airborne seedlings and the great white owl.

Micheleen peers through the small hole in the castle door, scanning the overgrown walls for the owl's nest. After careful study, the dried straw of the roost appears in contrast to the otherwise green growth covering the nooks and crannies of the respectable old structure. Two golden yellow eyes stare back at Micheleen. The stony stare rattles her, but she does not look away. She whispers, more to herself than to the owl, "Please don't scare Maeve anymore. I need her to like it here." The owl blinks slowly, then closes his eyes.

Micheleen returns to the car where Maeve remains hunkered down in the back seat. She opens the door and crouches down until she is face-to-face with her daughter. "Maeve, the owl is sleeping. Come on out so we can walk over the little bridge and down to the river path."

Maeve ignores her.

"C'mon, we might be able to see some bunnies there!"

That catches Maeve's attention; she sits up straighter and looks at her mother intently. "Bunnies? Real ones?"

"Yes, hundreds of them."

Maeve hesitantly clutches her tablet and creeps from the car, warily watching for the dreaded owl. She gingerly takes her mother's hand.

When Maeve exits, Micheleen spies Josephine's beloved hat balled up in the back seat. She considers returning it to the cottage, then thinks better of it, for fear of stirring the owl. She decides to tuck it in her coat pocket instead.

As the two of them walk toward the road, Maeve sneaks a peek back at the castle, keeping her mother to her word about that owl.

As they cross over the stone bridge, Micheleen stops in the middle and picks Maeve up. She carefully leans them both over the edge so they can watch the current flowing rapidly under the stone arches. Maeve hands her tablet to her mother. Micheleen beams, overjoyed that Maeve has willingly parted with what has become her security blanket since the divorce.

For the first time in a very long while, Maeve uses her hands to explore the feel of something other than a flat screen. She giggles as she examines the tiny little plants that poke their frond heads out from every crevice in the bridge's mortar. She runs her fingers across the mossy top stones. "Mommy, how can something be so rough and so soft all at the same time?"

Micheleen shrugs. A huge smile crosses her face as she watches her daughter delight in nature.

The rush of a cool wind sends Maeve cuddling up to her

mother. They stay like that for a while, embracing one another as they take in the beauty of the foreign land where the castle stands as tall as an old man can and the old woman of Slievenemon looks down and smiles.

Micheleen wishes her father could be here with them — that would make everything perfect. Micheleen looks down at Maeve and sees her clutching the necklace her own father gave her, a little gold heart hugging a sapphire birthstone. A look of sadness sweeps across the young girl's face. It breaks Micheleen's heart to know her daughter has a similar wish; it hurts even more to know that she's the reason it won't come true.

A large salmon leaps up from the Suir, startling them from thoughts about their fathers. The fish nearly reaches as high as their faces, catching them both off guard. "OOOOHH!"

Maeve takes a few steps back and points towards the water. "He tried to bite me."

"Oh, he did not!" Micheleen knows not to let Maeve revert to sulking, so she quickly changes the subject. "Hey! I think it's time to go find those rabbits."

Before Maeve can whine another word, the two of them scoot across the bridge to where the path along the river meanders on its way toward town. On the river walk, little brush wrens hop and flutter in and out of the edge growth.

"Look. Bunnies." Micheleen tells her daughter, knowing full well they are not. Maeve pretends to see rabbits with every rustle of weeds. Micheleen gleefully indulges Maeve's imagination.

"You know, Maeve, this is where leprechauns live. I wouldn't doubt if a couple of them are running around here too."

Maeve's eyes get big and round. "Really, Mommy?"

"Maybe. That's what Pop-Pop used to tell me." She shrugs her shoulders. "He said the leprechauns love hiding in the bushes because that's where they can see the most but be seen the least. And if you catch one, I think you get to make a wish."

Maeve looks down at her necklace. "You mean, I can wish for anything I want? And it will come true?"

Micheleen chuckles as she thinks about the Irish folklore that she grew up listening to. "Well, you have to catch one first. And I'm sure that's not easy."

Maeve crosses her arms in childlike wonder. "Why don't we have stuff like this back in America?"

Micheleen pauses to ponder the answer. "Hmm...Well, Ireland is an old country with a rich history. Before video games and computers, people would tell stories for entertainment, and those stories were passed down from generation to generation. I suppose some people might really believe in the stories, and others pretend for fun." Micheleen brushes her long, side swept bangs out of her eyes. "You should ask Auntie Jo to tell you some tales. Pop-pop always said she had the best ones."

Maeve's expression changes to a frown as she thinks about the old woman.

"Mommy, what do you believe?"

The question stops Micheleen cold as she wonders what it is exactly that she does believe in. Once she had believed in love, but that didn't work out so well. A hollow place in her heart calls out to be filled.

"I'm not sure, Sweetie. But I can tell you this – I believe there is something good out there waiting to be captured, and you and me are going to find it here in Ireland." She inhales deeply as she takes Maeve's little hand and continues walking down the path.

Maeve's eyes light up. "Will you help me catch a leprechaun?"

Micheleen revels at her daughter's excitement. "Well, I don't exactly know how. I think we'll have to talk to Auntie Jo about how to catch one."

Maeve's scowl returns. "I wish she would catch a cold... and die. Maybe then we could go home."

Micheleen gasps in horror. "Maeve! Don't ever wish for something like that! What if that came true?"

At the utterance of Maeve's morbid wish, a rabbit darts out of the bushes, scampering across their path and running off into the field. Both squeal with shock and delight.

"A bunny! A real bunny, Mommy!"

CHAPTER 7

Vespers Dashed

Father Adrian bows to the candlelit altar as he passes by to take his place in the side apse of the chapel. It is time for the friars to sing the sacred chant of The Magnificat, and his turn to lead.

As the men's voices bellow through the ancient chords, Father Adrian's thoughts are like a compass, constantly pointing toward Josephine. Her troubled expression and thoughts of death cannot be shaken. He pictures her hopeless expression and wonders if he should have done more.

Suddenly, he has an ominous flash, envisioning Josephine committing a most desperate act. His brow begins to drip with sweat and his skin turns clammy. Even though going against ritual and routine is against his nature, he believes within the depth of his being that Christ is asking him to help his lost sheep immediately. The fear of what could happen if he does not go to her aid begins to overwhelm him as he eeks out a final line of Latin, his voice cracking on the last note.

The other friars turn and look at Father Adrian, who usually has the voice of an angel. He whispers, "Forgive me, brothers," pale with dread, and excuses himself. Gasps and murmurs follow him as he sprints out the doors.

Father Adrian runs down the street in his long brown robes, a bizarre cross between Forrest Gump and an apostle. He dashes down to the river's path where he believes Josephine will be making her way to Castlecottage.

As he rounds the bend, he hears the frantic, high-pitched tones of a distressed American accent. Fearing the worst, he digs deeper and runs at a pace his body has never known. As he approaches the riverbank, he sees a tall brunette woman motioning erratically, first to a young girl standing on the shore, and then toward Josephine's distinctive cap, floating down the River Suir.

Fearing the worst, the priest flings himself into the current. He soars through the air like Superman in a chocolate-colored tunic. The two bystanders are aghast at the sight of this strangely dressed man appearing from nowhere, catapulting without warning into the cold water.

Father Adrian scrambles for the floating article, snatching it from the current as he stands, finding his legs. The water is thigh deep. He scans the river for Josephine and then calls out to the woman on the shore, "Quick! Call the Garda, we need help!"

The woman looks confused. "Help? We don't need any help."

She looks over at her daughter, then back to Father Adrian, likely wondering if the dripping man in holy attire has lost his marbles.

Father Adrian's heart is pounding as he struggles to catch

Father Adrian huffs as he storms off. *Argh, she's probably plannin' her own arrangements!*

Jimmy continues on his way, muttering, "More than his frock is soggy, I'd say."

Father Adrian quickly trails up the street leading to Kevin Whalen's. He stops under a sign engraved UNDERTAKER.

Micheleen and Maeve catch up as he opens the door. They walk in three abreast.

Lying straight out in front of them is the body of an elderly woman, her head obscured by a sheet. All three of them gasp in horror.

Maeve tugs on her mother's coat and whispers, "Is that Auntie Jo?"

A little man pops out from behind the sheet. "Ah, Father Adrian! Can I help ye?"

"Yes, we were told Josephine Byrne was brought here."

The mortician examines the looks on their faces and chuckles. "Well, she's not *here*." His eyebrows raise as his eyes dart down to the dead body in front of him.

"But a man said she was dragged into Kevin Whalen's," Micheleen says.

"Oh, sure! They dragged her in the *other* side for a drink." He motions to his left.

The thoroughly Irish concept of "undertaker and bar" escapes the American.

"Thank Jesus!" Father Adrian makes the Sign of the Cross and nods as he leads Micheleen and Maeve out the front door and on to the next entrance down. He leaves a trail of water all the way. "She must be trying to drown her sorrows."

The three make it to the next door, the one with the big sign saying 'BAR' overhead. The friar slowly opens the second door. As the three take a step inside, the dimly lit room renders them blind for several seconds. Their eyes adjust to reveal a pub filled with grinning faces. The first to come into focus, sitting front and center, is Josephine, pint in hand, with a gap-toothed smile as broad and craggy as the Kerry horizon.

Micheleen looks to Father Adrian, who is staring, mystified, at a happy Josephine. He walks up to Josephine, wet shoes squeaking with every step on the wood-planked floor. Each screech of his sandals draws the stare of more of the pub's patrons.

He extends his arm and presents the soggy blue hat to Josephine. Josephine takes it from him as he abruptly spins on his toe with an extended squeak and leaves the pub with his sopping tail between his wet knees.

When the door shuts behind him, the people return to their drinking.

Josephine looks to Micheleen for an explanation. "What's happened to my hat...and to Father Adrian?"

But before Micheleen can answer, Maeve tugs on her coat. "Mommy, was that lady next door dead?"

Micheleen stares blankly at Maeve and then back up at all the inquiring faces. "I think I need a drink."

CHAPTER 8

MUCH TO CARRY

With Josephine's damp and wrinkled cap fit snuggly back on its master's head, Josephine, Micheleen, and Maeve, each weighted down with grocery bags, make their way back to Castlecottage along the river path.

Micheleen recounts the valiant rescue of the drowning hat to Josephine as the old woman stifles a giggle. To think Father Adrian believed she would try to do herself in by drowning! No, Josephine's plans had been much less dramatic. She had planned on being found lying peacefully deceased in the soft, lush grass at the foot of the Holy Spot. Josephine's climb up her own bedroom stairs these days nearly does her in; the long, steep trek up to the grand Cross on the hill would surely result in her passing.

The beauty of the plan lay in its discretion; an innocent visit to the Holy Spot one last time would result in Josephine's death merely as a consequence of actions—far from suicidal, but effective all the same, God willing. If Immaculata had not crossed her path and forced her into the pub, Josephine would likely still be on her death march.

Josephine chuckles to herself. She knows full well it was Divine Intervention that changed her plans. The temptation of a pint with friends was too good to pass up.

She says a mental prayer of thanks to God for her weakness to sit on the high stool and asks His forgiveness regarding her selfish thoughts of dying on her own terms. Father Adrian had it right all along; God bless that brave, hat-saving priest.

Josephine pauses, slowly puts a bag down on the path, and touches her hat. "Nearly dry."

She bends to grab her bag, but Micheleen quickly scoops it up.

Josephine muses, "He must have thought ye were tryin' to kill me."

"What? Are you serious?"

"I'd told him about ye. He was suspicious, thinkin' you wanted my land."

Micheleen gasps. "I can assure you that our arrival has nothing to do with that! Father Adrian gave me the impression you were... resorting to something drastic."

"Drastic? Well, I suppose going to the pub for a pint is a bit drastic for me. I've not been in there since before Teddy took ill... more than three years ago now. I can't blame Father for thinkin' me a mess. I was a bit demandin' of him today. Not at all like myself."

Micheleen looks at the ground in shame. "Auntie Jo, I am so sorry we showed up here without you knowing we were coming. The past year has been crazy with Mom and Dad both dying, my divorce, and now my promotion here in Ireland. I haven't had much time to process any of it. I didn't think about how disruptive our arrival would be for you...We shouldn't have shown up like this." Micheleen shuffles her feet, and her expression turns solemn. "Maeve and I can stay at the hotel until we can find a place of our own."

"Have ye lost all of yer senses? A hotel? I'll hear none of it. Ye are family. Ye are stayin' with me." Josephine hears herself committing to what she genuinely wants no part of. She breathes deeply, blaming the pressure of her sister's ghost for sealing her fate with these long-lost relations. She looks up to the sky and shakes her head, "Maeve."

Meanwhile, little Maeve kicks a stone angrily behind them.

Micheleen peers into one of the bags. "Here you've gone and bought all this food and new linens and towels. I'm paying you for all of this, you know."

Josephine rearranges the three bags she is carrying. "Just make yer own beds. That's all I need from ye."

Micheleen notices Josephine struggling. "Auntie Jo, let me have those."

Josephine hands two more bags over to Micheleen, whose load is already quite full.

"How did you think you would get all of these bags home by yourself?"

Josephine smiles. "The leprechauns, of course."

Maeve's eyes get big, and she interjects from behind. "Real leprechauns?"

Josephine looks straight ahead with a most serious expression, "To be sure, real leprechauns."

Maeve struggles not to drag her bag, lifting it high for one moment before the weight gets the better of her. "Then why aren't they carrying them now?"

Josephine stops, turns around, and slowly stoops down to Maeve's level. "Ah, that's because I am with ye, and the likes of ye spooks them."

Maeve examines the woman in front of her with the wrinkled face and missing teeth. "You look spookier than I do."

Micheleen snaps, "Maeve!"

Josephine laughs, stuck in the stooped over position. "It's okay Micheleen, the wee one is right. I'm no oil paintin' anymore."

Josephine straightens and winces, then looks down at Maeve. "The truth is Maeve, it's yer smell...all that technology leaves an odor on a soul that the fairies and leprechauns will have none of."

At that moment, Micheleen's cell phone rings. Josephine nods, "That's exactly what I'm talkin' about."

Micheleen tries not to drop her bags as she scrambles for her phone in a remote jacket pocket.

"Hello? Yes...yes. Well, I was hoping for a couple days to get settled, but I understand. ...Ok, but I will need to line up childcare for tomorrow...Oh, really? That's great, thank you. Can't wait to meet with you tomorrow as well...Good-bye." Micheleen punches a button and reaches down to pick up her grocery bags.

"Well Auntie Jo, it looks like I have to start work tomorrow." Micheleen sighs. "Apparently, they have a daycare facility at the office, so I'll take Maeve with me until I can get her registered for school. We'll probably be out of the house before you even wake up."

As nice as a solo day to herself sounds, Josephine imagines her sister rolling over in her grave upon hearing that her great-grandchild is going to be left with strangers all day.

Josephine glances over. "Ah, that's nonsense! You won't find that in a boutique." She flaps her hand at the Americans. "Maeve, you've found a leprechaun shoe."

Maeve's eyes light up and her jaw drops. "Really? I did!?... Cool! I can't wait to tell Daddy!" She runs ahead toward Castlecottage with a newfound exuberance in her step.

"Maybe Ireland is starting to grow on her," Micheleen chuckles at the sudden change in her daughter's demeanor.

Josephine looks to the sky. "Should start to rain at any moment." No sooner had the words left Josephine's mouth than it started to sprinkle.

Micheleen is amazed. "How did you know that was going to happen?"

"At my age, the unexpected gets a wee more predictable." She thinks about the last eight hours and then adds, "... Sometimes, that is."

They quicken their pace as they scurry over the old stone bridge and down to the tree-lined drive leading to Castlecottage. Maeve is standing at the end of the path looking toward the castle keep. "Look, a rainbow!"

The three of them stop in the rain to take in the sight of the glorious rainbow arcing over the top of the cottage, like a page from a fairytale book.

Josephine studies the bands of color. "Ah, they're looking ye over Maeve."

Maeve looks from the rainbow to Josephine, and then looks around in all directions. "Who is looking at me?"

"Well, the leprechauns, of course. Ye must not smell as bad now that the rain's washed the video box from ye." Josephine chuckles. "Come now, let's get inside."

Josephine opens the door and ushers Micheleen inside. Maeve looks one last time at the rainbow.

"Make note of where it ends, Maeve. We can go searchin' fer the gold there tomorrow if ye like?"

Maeve studies Josephine and then runs to the safety of her mom without a saying a word.

CHAPTER 9

MAEVE'S MISERY

During dinner, Maeve cannot stop thinking about being stuck at home tomorrow with the elderly relative she barely knows. Although learning about leprechauns and looking for a pot of gold sound fun, she concludes it's probably best just to play her tablet most of the day.

After they've all finished eating, Micheleen begins to clear the table. Auntie Jo begins to get up as well.

"Uh, oh no, Auntie Jo, you just sit there and relax. Maeve and I will get the dishes. Maeve, bring me those glasses."

Maeve gets up immediately and begins to carry dirty plates to the sink.

Auntie Jo sits reluctantly, obviously wanting to do the work herself, but in too much pain to resist. She did more walking, lifting, and drinking today than she had in years.

A cell phone rings, startling the old lady. Micheleen, elbow deep in suds, calls out over her shoulder, "Can you get that Auntie Jo?"

Josephine hesitantly picks up the vibrating phone and stares at it blankly, turning it around in her wrinkled hands.

"Give it to Maeve. Maeve, honey, answer it before it goes to my voicemail."

Maeve curtly takes the phone from the clueless septuagenarian and presses the green icon on the screen.

"Hello? Oh, Daddy!" The biggest smile of the day creeps across her face. "Uh-huh, we're here in Ireland."

The happiness quickly turns into a frown. "No, I want to go home."

Her mother grabs the phone with a soapy hand. "James? I told you I'd call you…yes, but she needs to get ready for bed now. We are five hours ahead of you. Call back in a few days, once we've had a chance to settle in…She's fine. It's late. She's tired. You can talk to her more then. Okay? Okay…bye." She hangs up by jabbing the screen pointedly.

Maeve turns beet red, and she purses her lips. "But I'm not tired, Mommy! I want to talk to Daddy!"

Her mother takes a deep breath. "Maeve, it's late. Go get your pajamas on." Maeve stands there with her hands on her hips. "Now!"

Maeve reluctantly marches to her new room to change for bed. She can tell Mommy is rattled, but she isn't sure why. She never used to get like this around Daddy, but ever since their divorce was finalized, she's been acting weird.

The hallway looks creepier in the dark. She quickly makes her way to the bedroom and turns on the light. She looks from one end of the tiny space to the other. Her old room back in America was twice this size with a soft fluffy rug to wiggle her toes in. It was the prettiest shade of pink, not this booger green. *Yuck.* She had tons of toys back home, a television, and her own computer. Here, she has none of that. And worst of all, she doesn't have Daddy.

The bedroom is small and cold, but what bothers her most is the statue of the long-haired man on a wooden beam right over the bed. It's just like the one over the fireplace in the other room. *Why doesn't he have more clothes on?*

She climbs up on the bed and stands to take a better look at him. Up close, she realizes he is bleeding all over the place! Blood is on his hands and his feet, from his side where he has a big cut, and even from his head where these awful thorns are stuck all the way around! *Why would that old lady want a thing like this hanging in her house!?*

This place gives Maeve the creeps. She lies down on the bed and starts to cry. She puts her hands over her eyes and buries her face in the stiff pillow. As the fabric becomes wet with her tears, it begins to smell sweet, but Maeve doesn't want to acknowledge anything is sweet or nice here in Ireland. She just wants to go home.

She turns over and cries some more.

Through her tears, she notices for the first time a statue of a lady dressed in long blue and white robes standing on the vanity in the corner. *Is that the Queen of Heaven like the one back in that restaurant?* Something about her draws Maeve in. She wipes her eyes with her sleeve and gets up to take a closer look.

The woman is holding a blue necklace, just like the one Auntie Jo has hanging on the wall in the kitchen. *Maybe people in Ireland don't put necklaces on their necks?*

She runs her fingers along the cool, glassy beads and then looks back to the bleeding man hanging on the wall. Maeve starts to feel sorry for him, but she still wishes he weren't hanging right over her bed. She looks back to the pretty robed lady, whose smile feels real. Maeve grins momentarily before returning to her child-like misery. She wants to go home, and she wants her mom and dad together again.

Maeve doesn't understand why her mother is choosing to live in this creepy house instead of in a beautiful home with her dad.

She reaches up and runs her fingers over her healed scalp. *I hope that Auntie Jo's powers heal hearts too. Mommy's heart needs to love Daddy again.*

CHAPTER 10

NOT SO LUCKY, LUCKY DAY

 Micheleen finishes the dishes and takes a seat next to Josephine by the hearth.

 "Auntie Jo, I'll be leaving at the crack of dawn tomorrow to meet the plant supervisor. But there's no need for you to get up early. Maeve will fix herself cereal. The company's technician is going to come here to set up the computers. Maeve can let him in. And don't feel like you and Maeve need to stay here. Go do whatever you want to do. Maeve can help you run errands."

 Josephine wrinkles her nose at the thought of computers being brought into her home.

 "Yer so like yer Granny, that ye are. She, too, moved into my house a single mother... though she'd *lost* her man, not *left* him."

Micheleen's shoulders slightly slump at the remark. The awkward silence is clipped by Josephine's turn of tack, "Yes, just like her. She immediately started with all her modern conveniences talk and the nonsense just like yerself. She's the one who pushed for the electric lights and the silly indoor loos. All it meant was more bills to pay and more cleanin' to do. Can't say I see the convenience in that!"

Micheleen straightens in her chair. "But Auntie Jo, it's not just about convenience, it's for your safety! You need a cell phone so that we can easily get ahold of each other." She smiles and pats Josephine's knee. "But don't worry, it's going to be pre-programmed, so you won't have to do a thing!"

"If I don't have to do a thing, why have it at all?" Josephine rolls her eyes and shakes her head as the cell phone rings again.

Micheleen glances at the screen before putting the phone back in her pocket.

Josephine chimes in again. "What do I need a bloody mobile phone for? That thing chimin' non-stop, it's sure to drive me loony, that it would."

"It won't ring much. I'll be the only one calling you. And really, it's more for you to call me, in case of an emergency or something. Trust me, you'll grow to love it."

"Don't know if I'm ready fer so much love."

Micheleen laughs at the old woman's sarcasm, studying her shabby dress, haphazard white hair, and the unmade face with its gap-toothed smile.

"Auntie Jo, once things settle down, I'm lining you up to come into the cosmetic plant's salon for a total make-over. We'll get your teeth worked on, and maybe do a little anti-aging therapy to brighten up your skin tone. When was the last time you had your hair done? I think a hint of blonde would look good on you. You've got great bone structure. And with the new clothes I'll design for you, people won't recognize you! What a 'before and after' you'll be." Micheleen clasps her hands together in excitement.

"Before and after? After Hell freezes over, that is." Josephine sits up as straight as her curved spine allows. "I've no need fer such foolishness. Anti-aging nonsense! Ye can't stop time. And I'm *thankful* fer my age. Ye can keep the false teeth, false lashes, and new wardrobe. I'll take my wrinkles, white hair, and old clothes just as they are. I'll take myself."

Josephine eyes Micheleen's perfectly groomed hair, applied eye lashes, and flawless foundation. "Ye really are yer granny all over again, pushing fer change. Ye know, not all change is good."

Micheleen ignores the advice, convinced that this move will bring the healing she needs. "Am I really like Granny? Dad told me some about her over the years, but not enough to make her seem real." Her expression turns solemn. "I wish I could have been able to get to know her."

Josephine's expression softens. "Oh, ye must be the head of yer mother with those brown eyes and All-American smile, but ye are my twin sister, yer Granny Maeve, in spirit."

"I didn't know you and Granny Maeve were twins?"

"Not regular twins, Irish twins. But we were more special beyond that. Most Irish twins are babes born within the same twelve-month period, yet few are like yer granny and me, separated by an exact twelve months. Brought to this earth on the same calendar day, that we were! On my first birthday my sainted mother gave me my first and best present ever, my darlin' sister, Maeve." Josephine's eyes become moist. "With all her trouble, yer granny was an angel to be sure, makin' work for me always under the pretense of betterin' things for me. She was a true charmer just like yerself. Ye know, today is the anniversary of her death?"

Micheleen's mouth falls open. "On May 21st?! No, I...I did not realize that."

Micheleen thinks back to what this day has meant to her for the last fifteen years and the reason for scheduling her arrival in Ireland on this very day. May 21st was her day of new beginnings. It was the day she graduated top of her class from Douglas S. Freeman High School. The day the local newspapers did a front-page story on Micheleen Kelly—the only student that year from Richmond, Virginia, to be accepted into Yale on a full academic scholarship. The one and only time she saw her father cry.

"Auntie Jo, how many years ago did Grandma die?"

"Fifteen years to the day."

Micheleen gasps. "That was the day of my high school graduation!"

During her Valedictorian address, Micheleen remembers looking to her father. His cheeks were streaming with tears. All these years she thought they were tears of pride and joy for her, his only child... but were they?

Micheleen looks at Josephine, "Do you know why my father didn't come back for Granny's funeral?"

Josephine hesitates and shifts uncomfortably in her seat. "I believe your mother needed him to help during your graduation festivities."

"But it was his own mother! How could he not be there?! He could have left right after my graduation and made it here in time for the funeral."

"Micheleen, yer father was in a difficult position."

"I don't understand…why?"

Josephine rubs her hands together in her lap and exhales slowly. "Yer dah was destined to leave Ireland. There was no fittin' future for his likes here. Michael was ambitious, smart, and good-looking. Ireland was just too small and too poor. He was like yer Gran, always up for the bigger and the better. She loved that about him. He was tailor made fer America and all it offered. He went to the U.S. and never looked back. He met yer mam and fell head over heels."

"But why did he have to sever his ties to his family here?"

"Well, when yer Granny went to America to visit yer dah and meet yer mam, I'm afraid it didn't go so well."

"Between Mom and Granny?"

"Yes, your mam not being religious was something yer Granny was willing to accept as long as ye were raised Catholic. Unfortunately, yer mam was to have no religion whatsoever in her household. When yer Granny brought ye a little Celtic cross, yer mam took it as if to save it for you when ye were older. But yer Granny found it pitched in the wastebasket. Goes without saying she confronted yer dah. Since yer mam had been raised Baptist and yer dah Catholic, they agreed to not raise ye religious at all, the conflicts just not worth the confrontin'."

"I didn't know there was that much difference between being Baptist or Catholic? Honestly, I don't know about religion at all. Is there really that much of a conflict?"

"Oh, in those days, and even still today in some parts, Catholics and Protestants are not to mix. Pure silliness, I say. However, yer Granny was royally upset about the cross being in the trash. Being true to her red-headed nature, she let yer mam know exactly what she thought of her. And then that was that."

"So, Dad picked Mom over Granny?"

"More that he picked his future over his past. Yer mam and dah loved each other very much. No marriage is easy. They may have made choices I wouldn't make, but they made them together and stuck with them. That's something to admire. That's what makes a true marriage. Thick AND thin. That's what vows are for. Convenience is not the point of takin' vows."

Micheleen's gaze hollows. She steers the conversation back to the necklace. "I wonder what happened to the little cross?"

"Hold on a moment."

Josephine gets up and goes over to the great hutch in the corner. She pulls open a small drawer. Fishing about, she extracts a small gold Celtic cross on a delicate gold chain.

"Better late than never."

Micheleen takes the cross from Josephine's knobby hand. She admires it for its simplicity. *How could Mom be so fearful of such a lovely little cross?*

Micheleen tears her gaze from the memento and looks back to Josephine. "This answers a few questions. Thank you for telling me. And thank you so much for this." Micheleen clutches the cross delicately in her hands.

"Thank yer Granny fer the cross. I'm glad to give ye answers, but be aware, one answer can bring on two questions in its wake."

blue rosary beads on their night-time perch. She shuffles out of the kitchen and up the hall.

The letter of the impending American invasion lies unopened on the front table. Josephine picks it up and tears open the seam. As she pulls out the letter, a photo falls to the floor. Josephine steadies herself with the table as she bends down low yet again. She picks up the picture and turns it over. It is a shot of little Maeve, a child so happy, smiling, and full of fun. The face beams back at Josephine. Josephine takes it over to the old photo of her and her sister, Maeve, as young girls. The face of Josephine and this little Maeve do look interchangeable. The joy in their eyes and the laughter coming right out of the photos is infectious.

Josephine studies them feature for feature. "Immaculata McClure needs her eyes examined. Not a bit of resemblance, I say."

Josephine lowers the snapshot and leans closer to the old photo on the wall, speaking to her sister. "Maeve, I miss ye. Even from the grave, yer here pushing me for my own good, just like ye use to do. Good night, Dearie. Good night."

Josephine crosses herself one more time and puts out the hall light before going upstairs for a much-earned night's rest.

CHAPTER 11

OLD BONES

Josephine opens her eyes to the shafts of sunlight tickling her eyelashes. From under her bedsheets, she starts to rise, but finds her body is locked in place. Every joint and muscle is frozen. She raises her head half an inch off the pillow. The weight of her own head gets the better of her, and she plops it back down again.

"Micheleen! Micheleen!"

Josephine picks her head up enough to read the clock by her bedside – 7:43. She realizes Micheleen has been gone to work for well over an hour. She tries one more time to maneuver her body to its usual morning hoist position, but again, no luck.

Josephine glances up to the bedpost. How can this be the same body that used to jump and bump and swing around the bedposts of this bed as a child with her sister and two brothers? Now this body could not reach that bedpost to save her soul. She takes a deep breath, "Maeve! Maeve, come up here! Maeve, wake up! I need ye!"

Maeve wakes up to the sound of someone croaking her name. Groggily, she rolls over, not sure where she is.

"Maeve!"

Maeve squints around, remembering she's in Ireland and that her mother has already left for work. It must be old Auntie Jo calling her.

"Maeve, wake up! I need ye!"

Maeve begrudgingly crawls out of bed, obeying the desperate calls and making her way up the creaky stairs to Auntie Jo's bedroom. Peeking inside the door, she sees nothing but an old, white-haired head peeking just over the top of the blue-ticked bed sheets.

"Maeve, I'm stuck."

Maeve stares at her incredulously. "How are you stuck?"

"My bones aren't working. Here, take my hand."

One talon emerges from under the sheets, outstretching slowly toward Maeve. Maeve closes her eyes for a moment, flinching, then moves toward the bed. Reluctantly, she reaches for the elderly appendage, grasping it.

"Now pull me forward."

Maeve begins to pull on the brittle hand.

"Oh, no, don't squeeze so hard!"

Maeve eases up then tries again with a lighter grip. Auntie Jo winces but grits through the tug. Finally sitting upright, she exhales. "Now, pull my covers back so I can swing my legs over the side."

Maeve peels the linens back, revealing two spindles covered by a faded floral night-dress. The child is torn between laughter and disgust at this absurd sight. She never imagined old people in their nightclothes would be funny to see, but something about it is...very funny. Maeve does her best to keep her serious expression, all the while nurturing her silent giggles.

"Maeve, now swing my legs over."

Squeamishly, Maeve latches on to the skin covered twigs.

"Easy, not too fast now."

Auntie Jo is finally in her up-and-out position. She reaches an arm for the bedpost to steady herself while grabbing on to Maeve's arm with the other. "Okay, girl, this is going to be a trick. On the count of three....one, two, three! UHHHHH!" Auntie Jo pushes as Maeve pulls. In one fluid movement, the old woman is up and on her feet. "Ah, that's grand now. Well done, Maeve, well done."

Maeve stands there, examining Auntie Jo in her sack of a nightgown. The comparison everyone makes of Maeve to this bag of bones seems even more unlikely than it did yesterday. Maeve promises herself she will never look like *that*, no matter what.

Auntie Jo gets her sea legs moving as she slowly lets go of Maeve's arm. Maeve's face is a mixture of disbelief and repulsion as she witnesses the plight of old age itself.

"Okay, go on to the kitchen. I'll be down shortly to fix ye some breakfast."

Maeve retreats as fast as she can, hoping to never see Auntie Jo in her pajamas again.

Josephine turns her head to the mirror at her vanity, taking in the sight Maeve just witnessed. Bushy, white hair all askew; a nightgown draping her frail, curved body; knobby hands and feet, twisted and swollen at each joint; and a mouth sprinkled with teeth. A sight indeed.

Josephine grins at the aged reflection and chuckles. *Surely Maeve agrees that we share no resemblance.*

CHAPTER 12

FRIAR INFIRM

Father Adrian files into the sacristy for morning prayers. His brother friars enter silently amongst the shuffling of feet and the whoosh of robes. Father Adrian dips his fingers in the holy water to bless himself.

A friar behind him whispers, "Don't fall in, Adrian."

Snickers ripple down along the line of brown hoods.

Adrian ignores them and takes his place in the pew. Even in the ranks of the holy robes, schoolboy ribbings are alive and well.

Adrian joins in the familiar Gregorian chants when, suddenly, he drops his prayer book, making a loud thump amongst the chants. Again, all eyes and whispers target the disjointed friar. He bends down to pick the book up. A red-hot pang surges up his spine, wrenching his back to the point that he is unable to right himself. He tries to muffle his shrieks of pain. The two friars flanking Father Adrian attempt to help him. He cries out in excruciating agony, calling the morning prayers to an awkward halt.

Adrian is ushered out, moaning as the rest of the Friary and the pastor, Father Sean, look on in curious, albeit concerned, astonishment. For the second time in less than 24 hours, Father Adrian has brought a sacred service to a standstill. Rumors of a mental breakdown and even demonic oppression begin their rounds.

Adrian lies in the fetal position on his priestly cot. Not only is pain radiating up his spine, but each knuckle aches, as do the joints in his wrists, elbows, and knees. Doctor McQuirk enters the darkened cell with Father Sean.

The doctor carefully feels along the priest's spine. He examines the swollen hands and joints, then looks to the face of Father Adrian. "How long have ye been in pain?"

"Since I bent over to pick up a book in mornin' prayers."

"Yer hands weren't bothering ye before this?"

"No, but since my back went out, I've noticed the pain in my joints as well."

Dr. McQuirk turns to the pastor in a hushed tone, "I'm not quite sure what to make of it, but it looks to be an advanced case of rheumatoid arthritis."

Father Sean pulls back from the doctor, "Can't be. He was standin' straight and tall without an ounce of pain just this mornin'."

The doctor shrugs his shoulders. He looks back down at the pain-riddled priest. "I heard he's been in the Suir yesterday, true?"

"Yes."

"Could be some sort of virus he picked up from the river. It came on a bit quick, but tha 'tis a possibility. The virus could be causin' inflammation to his joints." He stoops so his face is over Father Adrian's.

"I'm giving ye an anti-inflammatory. It should bring the swellin' down. Till then stay in bed, man!"

Father Adrian wrinkles his nose, "Thank the Lord for doctors' invaluable instructions." He winces again.

CHAPTER 13

OLD MEETS NEW

Josephine whizzes down the stairs to the sound of dishes clanking in the kitchen at the far end of the cottage. She whisks by the hallway photos, her feet deftly carrying her over the wood floors. Fearing a mess, she rounds the corner to find Maeve standing in a puddle of milk on the floor.

"Oh, Maeve, here now, let me wipe that up with a wet towel." Josephine quickly tends to the mess. She hands the cereal bowl to Maeve. "Here Dearie, take yer breakfast and go sit at the table to eat."

Maeve makes her way to the table and begins eating her cereal while Josephine nimbly swoops down to wipe up the white droplets. Maeve looks at Josephine with a confused and astonished expression.

"Wha 'tis it, child? Why are ye lookin' at me like that?"

Maeve looks down at her bowl of cereal.

"C'mon now. Spit it out."

Maeve swirls the spoon around in the creamy milk. "Well...I was just...I was just wondering if you're a witch, and if you did a spell on yourself so you could move better."

Josephine halts her mopping for a moment, letting this sink in. Her movement *is* freer than it typically is at this point in the morning, especially without her first sips of pepper tea.

"No spell. I'm a healer, NOT a witch. But even so, my gift is from God to use only for others, not myself."

Josephine attributes her unusually free movement to the rush of adrenaline she experienced in the face of needing to save her clean and tidy kitchen.

"By the way Maeve, thank you for helping me out of bed."

Maeve nods, taking another spoonful of Flakies. She enlists the tablet with her free hand and begins playing a game amongst bites.

Josephine hears the first pings and zings of the day. She closes her eyes and grumbles as she begins making her tea.

"Ye'll never see a leprechaun playin' with that wretched thing."

Maeve reaches the next level of her game. "If you don't do magic, how do you know so much about leprechauns?"

"I know about leprechauns and how to make 'em grant wishes fer that matter, but that has not the faintest thing to do with magic."

A cell phone sounds from the other end of the kitchen, rattling Josephine.

"What the divil? Is that yer mother's mobile makin' that terrible sound? She must have left it here to be able to call us from the office."

Maeve looks in the direction of the chime.

"Answer it, Maeve. I can't work that cruel thing."

As Maeve gets up to answer the phone, the doorbell rings.

"That one I know how to answer," Josephine says as she makes her way to the door.

At her doorstep is a burly, uniformed workman with laptop in hand and an assortment of wires to boot. "I'm here for the installation."

"Ah, must ye?"

Maeve comes running up to the man with the cell phone to her ear. "Mommy, he just got here. Is the laptop mine? Yay!"

Maeve gives the cell phone to the workman. He listens to Micheleen's instructions, confirming that he has Josephine's completely programmed phone.

"Yes, I'll go over how it works with her. Sure, she'll call ye as a test."

The workman hands the phone back to Maeve. "Yer mam wants to talk to ye, but first tell me, which one is yer room?" Maeve points in the direction of the green crucifix room.

Josephine's head is spinning with this inundation of electronics.

Having dropped off the laptop and wires in Maeve's room, the workman returns holding out a brand-new silver cell phone in front of Josephine's face. It looks exactly like the phone Micheleen uses.

"Mum, I'll show you how yer phone works before I get goin' on the computers."

"*My* phone? I have no use for that unholy thing."

"It will just take a moment; it's all programmed for ye."

Josephine knows he is just doing his job and takes mercy on him.

"Come here, Maeve, and listen to what he's telling me. At least *ye* will know how to work it."

The workman begins by showing Josephine the different ring tones to choose from. He pulls up the first. "Here's what they call STORM."

A techno rock noise pulses from the phone. Josephine rejects this straight away.

"Oh heavens, no."

He goes for the second. "This is called PASTA RASTA".

A reggae jam begins. Josephine wrinkles her nose.

"That pasta 'tis overcooked. Next."

The workman tries a third.

"Here's the tone ROMANCE." *Some Enchanted Evening* rings out and Josephine's eyes soften.

"That one will do."

Maeve's face squinches in disapproval of Josephine's choice.

The workman programs the tune for her calls then shows her how to dial Micheleen from her 'Favorites' list.

"Let's give it a go then," he says.

Josephine clicks on Micheleen's name and holds the phone to her ear.

"Hello?..Auntie Jo?"

Josephine listens to the voice on the other end, stunned.

The workman stares at Josephine.

"Tisn't anyone answerin'?"

"Oh, yes, yes Micheleen? I'm here, are ye there? He's showin' me and Maeve how this contraption works."

Micheleen responds, "Good, now go ahead and do whatever you need to do, but make sure to bring the phone with you.

Liam will be there for the next several hours wiring. Just leave him there to finish."

"Okay, Micheleen. Goodbye then."

Josephine holds the phone out to Liam, who punches the end call button.

Liam completes the tutorial by showing Josephine the texting feature.

"Don't bother, I'll never use such a thing. These old fingers can barely push a doorbell, let alone bang out a message on that puny device."

Liam and Maeve exchange raised eyebrows.

"Very well, then, do ye have any questions?"

Josephine shakes her head while she holds the cell phone in her hand, examining the foreign object.

Liam leaves to load more wires and computer hardware into Maeve's room.

Josephine's phone starts to play *Some Enchanted Evening*. "Ah, what tis it I do, Maeve?"

"Push the green button!"

"Right."

Josephine pushes the screen surface gingerly with her wrinkled finger.

"Ah, hello? Yes, 'tis working. We'll be heading out shortly. Fine."

Josephine holds the phone towards Maeve.

"Maeve?"

"Push the red button."

Josephine pushes it, and then stares at the array of hieroglyphics that pop up after. "Argh!", she says as she lays the phone down on the counter next to Micheleen's.

"C'mon, Maeve, we need to go into town. Get yer jacket and hat, and we'll be off.

Josephine puts on her own jacket and hat, then reaches for her rosary. "Jesus, Mary and Joseph, where's my rosary?" She bends down and scours the floor, pulling up the rugs, looking behind the sideboard frantically.

"Maeve, help me find my rosary. I know I hung it here last night…or did I? That pint may have fooled me. I'll check my room. Ye keep lookin' about the floor fer it."

Maeve puts her hands to her chest.

Josephine looks at her and notices something bulging under Maeve's shirt around her collar.

"What's that ye have on?"

Maeve does not answer, instead choosing to silently remove the rosary from her person. She hands the sparkling blue beads over to Josephine.

Taking the rosary, Josephine explains, "Maeve, yer not to wear a rosary around ye neck. It's not mere jewelry, did yer mam never tell ye that?"

Maeve shakes her head.

Josephine looks Maeve up and down.

"Do ye know what this is for?"

Maeve again shakes her head.

"Dearie, the holy rosary is the storehouse of countless blessings. It is a precious guide to help ye say yer prayers; yer Hail Marys and yer Our Fathers, so ye don't lose count.

Maeve looks confused.

"Maeve, have ye ever gone to church?"

"No."

"No?! Well, today you're going to church to pray for your

mother and father. Grab yer hat and leave that bloody game here. No electronics in Mass."

Maeve scowls at the thought of leaving her tablet behind.

"Well, ye want them back together, don't ye?"

Maeve's eyes brighten a bit, but she looks at Josephine hesitantly.

"C'mon, Dearie. Let's go."

Maeve reluctantly puts her tablet down and grabs a cell phone from the counter.

"Maeve, I said no electronics."

"But Mommy said to keep it with you when we went out," the girl protested.

Josephine remembers she did agree to this.

"Well, if we run into a leprechaun, don't let him know we have this."

She grabs her handbag, puts the cell phone in it, and scoots with Maeve out the back door.

The sky is overcast, and a light drizzle fills the air. Despite the less than sunny day, Josephine feels a spring in her step and a strength in her stride that she hasn't felt in years. If she did not know better, she would swear she was standing a good two inches straighter than she was the day before.

Maeve isn't sure about this need to go to church. "Auntie Jo, why do we have to go to church to do this praying?"

"We should pray to God at all times, but visiting with God in His house is the best way to thank Him."

"For what?'

"Fer lovin' and thinkin' of us so much."

Maeve looks down at the ground.

"He doesn't think of me. He doesn't even know me."

"Oh, but He does Maeve, more than ye know yerself."

"But how?"

"Well, fer one thing, He made yer soul and gave ye as a baby to yer mam to be with her, lovin' and carin' for ye till yer grown."

"Did he send me to my daddy too?"

"Yes."

"Then why can't I be with both of them?"

Josephine points a finger in the air. "That's the perfect thing to pray to God about when we get to church."

"Can God make Mommy and Daddy married again?"

"That's for ye to talk to God about. Ask Him when we get there."

Maeve pouts and scratches her chin. She kicks a rock and crosses her arms. If she is excited about going to church, she is hiding it well.

As the odd duo walk along the river path, Maeve gazes up to the mountainside, seeing a large white cross gracing the top of the hill. The sun shines on it, making it appear electrified in broad daylight.

"What's that white pole up there on the hill?"

Josephine looks for a pole, not realizing what Maeve is referring to. "What pole?"

Maeve points in the direction of the cross. "There."

"That's no pole, Dearie, that's the Holy Cross."

"Is it like the one that man is hanging on in my room?"

"Yes, the very same. That man is Jesus. Ye'll see Him when we get to church."

Maeve's eyes get wide. "Will he be praying for stuff too?"

"No, we pray to Him. He'll be on the Cross, like in your room."

"Oh."

Maeve frowns and looks up to the empty white Cross on the hillside. "That one is much nicer to look at, especially with those little white dots floating on the grass all around it."

"Those white dots are sheep, Maeve."

Maeve's mouth drops open. "Really!? Can people go up there next to it and see them?"

"Why of course! Ye just walk the path. It takes a while, but it is lovely up there."

Josephine feels the strength of her legs, the air in her lungs filling her with vigor; the sharp vice of arthritis has released, allowing movement with an ease she has not enjoyed in decades. Today a hike up to the Holy Spot will be anything but a death sentence.

"Would ye like to go?"

Maeve scrunches her nose, unwilling to attach herself in any way to her elderly relative. She kicks another rock. "Are there bunnies up there?"

"Gobs to be sure, and fairies too."

"What about leprechauns?"

"Leprechauns tend to venture to lower ground during the day. They are a whole different order than the fairies. Fairies stay in the higher spots, like by the Holy Cross. We'll get some sandwiches after Mass and head up there to eat. The weather should hold for most of the day."

Maeve hesitantly agrees.

As they near town, buildings begin to pop up from behind the bushes, revealing the quaint urban center nestled at the foot of rural green slopes. A huge gust of wind greets their faces, lifting Maeve's cap high into the air and down along the path from where they'd just come. Josephine holds her own hat firmly to her wild white hair.

"Oh, there goes ye cap. Quick, fetch it before it rolls into the river like mine did yesterday."

Maeve lets go of Josephine's hand, chasing her cap down the gravel path. It tumbles along before being swept away from the water and into the thick brambles on the other side of the path. Maeve follows the blue streak into the brush, but no cap is to be found.

"Auntie Jo! My hat is gone! It was here just a second ago, but I can't find it anywhere." Maeve shouts.

Josephine stomps back down the path and straight into the bushes where the cap disappeared. She, too, is engulfed in the brambles. Maeve watches from a distance for a few seconds before Josephine emerges with only her bulging purse in hand.

"Why, Maeve, I believe ye've had an encounter with a leprechaun. He took yer cap but left ye this evidence behind." Josephine points at a small shoeprint in the mud under the bushes. It appears to be the same size as the shoe found the day before.

Josephine pulls yesterday's shoe from her purse and places it next to the indentation. "Look. It's a match."

"But I want my hat back."

"He may give it back, he may not. But if ye see him, don't take yer eyes off him. Just stare right at him and demand all of his gold."

Maeve shouts. "I don't want gold! I want my hat! My Daddy gave me that hat."

"'Twas a lovely blue. But we have no time to track him down.

We must get to church to pay our respects to the saints before Mass starts."

Maeve shrugs her shoulders in an exasperated sigh as they march on up the path. She looks back over her shoulder, no blue cap in sight. "Why doesn't the leprechaun have to go to church, too?"

"They're of a different order of God's beings, they've not souls like ours. They're respectful of our faith, but are not called to worship as we do."

"Why not?"

"To tell ye the truth, I'm not sure. There are things we don't know about the leprechauns and fairies, as there are things they don't know about us. And there is even more that neither man nor wee folk know about God, but I suspect one day that part of the story will be made clear, and we can all have a good laugh over how simple and lovely it surely is."

Maeve shuffles her feet along the path as she thinks about all the scary stuff in Ireland, like Auntie Jo in her nightgown, the white owl, the thieving leprechaun, and Jesus bleeding on that cross. Her scowl turns to a bit of a smirk. *Ireland is a little scary, but it sure is exciting!*

Maeve and Auntie Jo enter through the Friary doors. The church is a cavernous place with ceilings that are too high to see to the top. The flickering light of the offertory candles bounce about the marble arches, dancing along the walls. The smell of incense is heavy as it wafts up to the invisible rafters. Little old people, some kneeling, some sitting, dot the pews. One old man is slumped over, snoring in prayer.

Auntie Jo leads Maeve over to the left side apse where a statue stands in front of a side altar. Auntie Jo touches her own forehead, chest, and then each shoulder with the fingers of one hand.

"Maeve, this is how ye make the Sign of the Cross."

She takes Maeve's right hand and shows her how to move her arm the same way.

"Ye say, 'In the name of the Father, the Son and the Holy Ghost,' then end with your palms together and say 'Amen.'"

They each do the Sign of the Cross while blessing themselves in front of the statue.

Maeve looks around hesitantly. "Do I start to pray to God now about my mommy and daddy?"

"Not yet, we're to make the rounds of the saints first. Then once that is done and we're in the pew, ye can start in with all of that to God. Do what I just taught you at each statue we go to and then let me say the rest."

Maeve exhales loudly. "How long is this going to take?"

Josephine ignores her question and ushers her to the first statue.

"Is that God?"

"Oh, heavens, no! This is St. Anthony. The saints were people like ye and me, but they lived their lives servin' God nearly perfect, at least by the end. We don't worship the saints; we ask for their intercession. We ask them to pray fer us because their prayers are powerful, and we use them as examples to learn, to serve, and to grow closer to God as they did. Do ye understand?"

Maeve nods timidly. "Can I start praying yet?"

Auntie Jo begins her prayer to St. Anthony. Maeve fidgets,

looking annoyed. Once said, they move on to St. Francis, following the same routine.

Next, the pair heads toward the main altar. Maeve looks up and sees a life-size Jesus hanging on an enormous cross. His wounds glisten as if the statue is truly bleeding. Behind Him is a spectacular stained-glass window shining with the colors of the rainbow, headed by golden rays.

Auntie Jo kneels nimbly in front of the altar. Maeve follows. She tugs on Josephine's pocket as she looks at the cross.

"Could your special cloth make Jesus stop bleeding?"

"Dearie, that isn't the real Jesus up there. It's a statue of Him, but His real Spirit is here all around us. The statue reminds us of that. But, to answer yer question, no, my cloth would not have stopped His bleedin'. His bleedin' was the will of God. Jesus died a brutal death as atonement for our sins so that we have the chance to spend eternity in Heaven with Him."

Maeve has a confused expression on her face. Her head swirls with millions of questions, but she knows if she asks them it may prolong her time at church, so she refrains.

They continue to the final statue to the right of the altar. Maeve recognizes her as the same beautiful woman from the restaurant and the dresser back at the cottage, but this time she is holding a baby. Maeve looks into the face of the statue and absorbs her smile.

Josephine blesses herself and begins to pray a Hail Mary.

Maeve points up to the statue, unable to hold back this question. "Is her name Mary?"

Josephine stops praying to answer, "Yes. She is our Blessed Mother. The Mother of Jesus."

Maeve's eyes dart back and forth between the baby in the

statue's hands and the man on the cross. "The same Jesus that's up there?"

"Yes. Jesus is the Son of God. He came to earth as a tiny baby through Mary. At every age and stage of His life, from the time he was in Mary's womb to His death on the Cross, He's the same Son of God."

"Is it time to pray for my parents yet?" Maeve asks impatiently.

Auntie Jo looks back to Mary, "We'll continue this later, Blessed Mother. Amen."

Auntie Jo points to a pew off to the side of the Virgin's statue. There they take a seat.

Auntie Jo pulls down the kneeler and kneels yet again. "Now ye can say yer piece to God. The Mass should not be starting fer another five minutes. When the priest comes in, stop yer praying. Stand, sit, and kneel whenever I do. The priest will do the rest."

"Auntie Jo, how do you know all of those words to say in front of the statues?"

"I was schooled by nuns who beat the prayers into us."

Maeve's eyes widen. "Beat?"

"Well, maybe 'beat' is a harsh word. The nuns instructed us intensely to learn the words, and I'm thankful they did."

"Do you have to say just those words for God to hear?"

"No, but if ye do learn the words to specific prayers, yer united with all sorts of people from all over the world, all prayin' with one voice. God listens to every word; however, when there is unity there truly is strength. When we all say the same words, it takes the different folk of the world and makes each person, rich or poor, brilliant or dull, able to leave their daily life for a moment and be lifted to the celestial plane of God, all together. But not to worry, Maeve, God wants to hear from ye whatever way ye want to speak to Him. Let's pray on our own now before Mass starts."

Auntie Jo blesses herself, as does Maeve. Maeve looks up to the altar and says loudly, "God, will you please make my mommy love my daddy again?"

Auntie Jo quickly claps her hand over Maeve's mouth.

The other old heads in the pews all turn to look at the boisterous petitioner.

"No, Maeve, yer to say yer personal prayers to God quietly, in yer own head, not out loud."

Maeve exhales loudly. "Then how is He going to hear me?"

"He's God, he hears yer heart. No need to use yer mouth."

Maybe that's why it's hard to hear God, because people don't talk loud enough to Him so he thinks He can't talk out loud either.

Maeve does as she's told and tells God what she wants inside her head and heart.

Josephine cuts her eyes to Maeve. The little girl has her eyes shut tight and her lips pursed with determination. Josephine smiles and goes back to her own sacred intentions.

Suddenly, from Josephine's satchel, a ringing pierces the air of prayer. It is not *Some Enchanted Evening*, rather it is the bell tone of Micheleen's phone. *Maeve must have picked up the wrong phone by mistake.*

Josephine fumbles for the incessant chiming, eventually finding it and handing it frantically to Maeve.

"Here! Answer it, quick!" She says in a hushed tone. The contingent of senior citizens is all ears.

Maeve presses the button on the screen.

"Hello?..Daddy!" She squeals and begins to jump up and down. "Wow! God really did hear me! Church works!!"

Maeve beams at Josephine and yells, "Auntie Jo, I can't believe it! God did it...It's Daddy!"

Josephine pushes her index finger to her lips. "Shhhssssh-hh—Maeve, come...talk to him outside."

Josephine grabs Maeve by the arm and hustles her down the aisle of the Friary while all heads turn to follow their exit. They finally make it out of the front door.

"Daddy, Auntie Jo and I are in church. I just told God that I missed you and wanted to talk to you. And then, you called! It works! You need to start praying, Daddy!"

More people file past Josephine and Maeve into church for Mass, keeping their straight faces.

"Shh. Dearie, not so loud."

Maeve continues her conversation with her father. "You are? When?!... I love you, Daddy. I can't wait! I'll tell her. Bye!" Maeve hits the end call button.

"Yer father, uh?"

"Yes. He's coming here to see me and Mommy!"

Maeve leaps over and hugs Josephine, smiling genuinely at her for the first time before grabbing her wrinkled hand. "Come on, we need to get back in there and pray a whole lot more!"

Josephine smiles at the change in Maeve's demeanor. "Wait a minute. Isn't there a button to turn that thing off? We can't have it chimin' in church again."

Maeve thinks for a moment. "I won't pray to talk to anyone else today, so it should be okay to turn it off."

Josephine spins Maeve back toward the church doors, saying under her breath, "Beginner's luck."

Josephine and Maeve return to their pew by the Blessed Mother. As they take a seat, Father Sean enters to prepare the altar. Josephine cocks her head.

"Why would Father Sean be conductin' Mass, not Father Adrian?"

"Is Father Adrian the guy who went in the water after your hat?"

"Yes, the very same. He always celebrates daily Mass. He'd sooner poke his own eye out before missin' a ritual. I hope yesterday has nothin' to do with this. I couldn't imagine Father Sean strippin' him of his duties fer that. He was just doing what a good priest should do. We'll have a word with the pastor after Mass, right Maeve?"

Maeve nods in agreement as Father Sean signals the attendees to rise.

CHAPTER 14

GUILT BY ASSOCIATION

Father Adrian is lying on his cot. A beam of sunshine peaks through the window, illuminating the darkly lit room. The commotion of shuffling feet stirs him from his drug-induced stupor.

"Josephine, is that ye?"

Father Sean, Josephine, and Maeve stand over him at his bedside. Josephine answers, "Yes Father, 'tis me."

As Father Adrian opens his eyes, he is met with a blurry image of white hair and a hazy form. His sight becomes sharper as he recognizes the small, snaggle-toothed woman. "Josephine, yer not dead?"

"Hah! That's what I keep askin' too."

Father Sean puts a hand on Josephine's shoulder, "He's still a bit confused from the painkillers."

He bends down close to Father Adrian. "Father, can ye hear me?"

Father Adrian tries to sit up.

Josephine and Father Sean assist him, propping a pillow behind his back to steady him.

The pastor asks, "How's yer back feelin' now, Adrian?"

"It's tight, Brother, but the pain has numbed. Sitting up is fine."

Father Sean continues, "Well...Josephine, I want you to show Father Adrian what it is ye can do."

Josephine stands up straight and nimbly bends over and touches her toes.

"Ah, Josephine, ye'll have to tell me yer workout regimen once I'm in better form again. Apparently, I'm not in the shape I thought I was!"

"No, Father, ye are in fine shape, but Father Sean thinks ye've takin' on my arthritis so as to free me up to do God's biddin'. And after seein' ye myself, methinks tis true."

Father Adrian looks at Father Sean in disbelief.

"Oh, go on! The doctor said my inflammation is probably a reaction to some virus I picked up in the river."

The pastor comes closer to Father Adrian's bedside. "I believed that was the explanation until I saw Josephine here. Adrian, this is more than any coincidence. Do ye think ye just happened to get arthritis on the same day it mysteriously disappears from Josephine? Yer doing the true work of Christ by suffering fer yer flock as ye heal them! It's a miracle."

Josephine gently picks up Father Adrian's hand, "I pray that ye give me my pain back. I'm accustomed to it, but not havin' my Father Adrian celebratin' Mass for me... that I'm not accustomed to. No offense, Father Sean, but an old woman gets set in her ways, and changin' priests at my age is just too disruptive."

Father Adrian tries to pull himself up straighter, but the muscles in his back knot up. "Ahh!"

The pastor rushes toward him. "I'm okay, I'm fine." He gently pulls his hand from Josephine's. "And yer healin' hands need not work for my relief. What I want to say, Josephine, is that giving this pain back to ye is not my desire nor should it be yers. If what ye and Father Sean say is true, with my condition and yer condition being some miraculous exchange, it's God's swapping of the pain, not mine. I prayed for yer good health, physically and spiritually. If this is the manifestation, I am overjoyed with God's work."

"He's absolutely right on that, Josephine," said the pastor. "God ordains this as His will. It's not to be meddled."

Josephine smiled. "Father Adrian, ye know the talk will be that ye are the faith healer now."

Father Adrian lifts his head at Josephine and looks her straight in the eye. "Guilt by association. Perfect." He collapses back down on the pillow and closes his eyes.

CHAPTER 15

Hike to the Holy Spot

Josephine and Maeve exit out the back of the Friary. Josephine looks at her watch. "We'll go get some sandwiches and take them with us to the Holy Spot. We can eat up there, and I'll tell you all about the fairies."

Maeve's eyes widen in excitement. Josephine smiles, remembering her own childhood infatuation with the enchantment of her home country.

Josephine peruses the menu board hanging over the tearoom counter.

"What sort of sandwich would ye like, Maeve? They have ham and I believe chicken salad today."

Maeve looks over the different bowls of side dishes and salads before landing her sights on the pastries at the far end of the counter.

"Can I have one of those chocolate covered things?"

Josephine follows Maeve's gaze to the delectable-looking treats. "Oh, the French call those chocolate éclairs. They are my favorite. I'll get ye one, but ye must eat a sandwich first."

"Do they have peanut butter & jelly?"

"No, I would say not."

"Hmm, what about cheese sandwiches?"

"That they do."

A teenage girl behind the counter asks, "Can I help ye, mum?"

"Yes, one cheese sandwich, one ham with salad on the side, two éclairs and two Tipperary waters. All boxed to go, please."

"Very good. Pay at the end of the counter."

Josephine and Maeve walk out of the sandwich shop, boxes in hand, and head up toward the Holy Spot. Along the way passers-by greet Josephine with, "How are ye keeping?" "You're looking well, Jo;" and an offer to "Stop by the bar tonight?"

Josephine had a taste of this welcome yesterday, but with her absence of pain, the greetings seem even nicer. Immaculata McClure is the next to cross their path on the way up the hill.

"Ah, Josephine. Two days in a row? The saints must be smilin'. Will we see ye in the pub again tonight? Was grand fun going over old times with ye yesterday."

"Perhaps. Maeve and I are headed to the Holy Spot to eat and see a few fairies if we can."

"'Tis a perfect day to see 'em. They can't help themselves when the weather is this breezy and mild. Do make yer way back to town if ye can. I'll be having a quiet pint at Whelan's by four."

"I'll see what the hike does to my legs and back. If I'm up to it, we'll see ye there."

Immaculata continues on her way. "That would be grand. Well, I'm off to run my errands. Have fun with the fairies, Maeve; give them my regards!"

Josephine and Maeve cross the River Suir via the bridge coming down from the Clonmel Arms where they first met just the day before. From there, they head up the mountain road, encountering the silent nods of a few old men walking their dogs. One in particular is crusty Jimmy McCann, a classmate of Josephine's and a daily Mass attendee.

"Auntie Jo, that is the man who told Father Adrian you were at the undertaker's," Maeve whispers.

Jimmy tips his hat to the ladies as they pass. Josephine feigns a smile to him, "Hello, Jimmy."

"Have ye a moment?"

Josephine and Maeve turn back around. Josephine whispers to Maeve, "He always has an excuse to talk, God bless him."

Josephine approaches the old man. "Yes, Jimmy, what is it ye need?"

Jimmy hikes up his left trouser leg exposing his latest outbreak of shingles.

"Ah, I see."

Josephine digs a pin out of her satchel. She pricks the pointer finger of her left hand, milking it for a trickle of blood. With her scarlet ointment she makes a ring around the affected area, circling it three times: "In the name of the Father, and of the Son, and of the Holy Spirit. That should do ye."

"How much do I owe ye, Jo?"

"The usual, say a prayer for my soul after ye go to Confession. That will do me fine."

"I'll be sure to go. Don't want what happened to Ronan to happen to me." Jimmy tips his hat to them one last time as Josephine and Maeve turn to continue their ascent to the Holy Cross.

Josephine amazes herself with her newfound stride. Up the road they climb. At each bend they stop to take in the view, watching Clonmel grow smaller. As they reach the end of the road, they straddle over a cattle gate and then leap over a deep, dark crevice in the hill.

"Maeve, this crevice is undoubtedly inhabited by a firbolg... or leprechaun."

"What's a firbolg?" Maeve looks up at Josephine with a childlike wonder.

"Well, I was about yer age when I first learned about them too. Your granny and I had been exploring and stumbled upon a fairy ring–"

Maeve interrupts. "Was it gold!?"

"Oh no, not that kind of ring." Josephine chuckles. "Fairy rings are circles of rocks where fairies have their meetins."

"Cool! Did you see the fairies?!"

"We sure did. Our nanna had taught us all about them, so we knew the whirls of color had to be fairies flyin' about."

"Are firbolgs fairies too?"

"No, they were driven to the hills when the Celts ran them off the fields for good. The fairies were none too keen sharin' their hills with the firbolgs. The fairies eventually took domain, with the firbolgs bein' relegated to the lowest of the burrows and crevices of the hills. However, as warrin' factions are want to do, there is always the odd couplin'. In this case, the crossing of fairy with firbolg. These pairings, though few, are the cause of the hybrid creature known commonly as a leprechaun."

Maeve listens intently as Josephine continues.

"Apparently, the union of a fairy and a firbolg can only result in a male child which favors the firbolg in all physical features of a stout build, ruddy complexion, potato-like facial features along with the firbolg unsophisticated manner. But this creature does always acquire from its fairy parent an array of mystical powers… that can be used for mischief or good, determined again on the temperament of the firbolg parent."

Maeve lies down and crawls to the edge of the crevice to have a look inside. Nothing but black.

"I like the fairies better. That's what I want to see."

"Ah, well their little covered wood is just beyond."

"Let's go!" Maeve runs ahead on the straightaway of the narrow dirt path. She gets to where the path bends back up the hill and stops to wait for Josephine. Josephine is keeping a remarkable pace, just not up to the level of an energetic 7-year-old.

"Come on, Auntie Jo!"

"I'm coming, Maeve. Believe me, this is fast fer the likes of me."

They round the bend and head up a steep incline, reaching another plateau and another stretch of straightaway.

"See up there, where the brambles curve over the top? That's the little covered wood."

Maeve peers inside the entrance. Brambles and roots grow in a perfect circle around a small tunnel that cuts through to a higher part of the mountain.

"Can we walk through?"

"Ye can, but ye'll need to wait fer me to walk the path up to ye at the other end."

"I want you to come with me."

"Oh, darlin', I can't crouch that far down. Father Adrian may have taken the pain in my joints fer a while, but I'm afraid my body is not up to the low stoop and crawl for that long a distance. Ye go on. It's wonderful inside. Yer granny and I use to run back and forth through the tunnel fer hours huntin' fairies."

"Did you ever catch one?"

"Oh no. Fairies aren't fer catching, they're fer seein'."

"Did you see any?"

"I saw my share. Now go."

Maeve looks up inside the tunnel of brambles and roots. Specks of light find their way through the limbs and leaves, making the tunnel undulate with illuminated polka dots.

"I think I can see some flying around!"

Maeve takes Josephine's hand as they both peer through the opening. Josephine nudges her on. "Go on through the covered wood. Ye'll love it!"

"No, I'll stay with you."

Josephine senses Maeve's apprehension. "Okay then, on we go."

The two make their way up to the final leg of the ascent. They round the next bend, and suddenly the giant white cross stands before them. For most of the walk, the cross had eluded them, being mostly out of sight. Its stunning and unexpected appearance is breathtaking.

"Oh, Auntie Jo, the cross!"

"'Tisn't it gorgeous?"

"It's so big. How did they get it up here?!"

"It was quite a sight. It was placed there durin' the Marian Year, 1953 in honor of the Blessed Mother. Nearly every man and boy in Clonmel helped get it up here. What a day that was. They even wired it for electric, so it glows on the hill come dark, though I think most of the bulbs are burned out at the moment. Look now, here's the back end of the covered wood."

Josephine points to a tiny opening in the branches, just big enough for two little girls to climb up through together. They walk over to the opening.

"Wow, that would be fun to slide down." Just at the lip of the upper opening, a lush bed of shade grass grows on the incline up and out of the Fairy Wood.

"Oh, it's a lovely slide. Yer granny and I used to slide down here over and over and over again. Give it a go, Maeve. I'll stand here and watch ye. Ye can do the slide then turn back and climb up. Ye need not go all the way to the other end."

Maeve ponders this suggestion, but she doesn't quite trust Ireland yet.

"No, I'd rather go up to the cross."

"To the cross, we go!"

Sheep run over the path in front of them as they make their way to the Holy Spot. Behind the cross is a tiny chapel and altar where outdoor Masses are sometimes held. The sheep bleat at Josephine and Maeve as they saunter over the field and up to the mighty cross.

"Shall we say the first trio of the rosary by the Cross before we eat?"

Maeve nods her head.

"Alright then." Josephine takes her blue rosary beads from her purse and hands them to Maeve. "Ye keep track of where we are. This first bead is for an 'Our Father,' then the next three beads are for 'Hail Marys.' When I start off with saying 'Hail Mary,' ye go to the next bead until we've said two. On the third bead, give me a nudge and I'll know to say one more 'Hail Mary.' Then we'll finish with a final 'Glory Be' and be done. Do ye have that?"

Again, Maeve nods.

"Good. In the name of the Father and of the Son and of the Holy Spirit. Amen"

Josephine begins.

Maeve takes her role as 'Hail Mary' tracker quite seriously. She focuses on the gleaming white cross looming over their heads as she squeezes her fingers tightly on the correct bead. Behind and above the cross, the sky is the bluest blue Maeve has ever seen.

A cool breeze blows her long, dark hair away from her face as she lets the silky grass under her knees cushion her moment of devotion. The sound of Auntie Jo's voice saying the prayers makes her feel calm and happy. The blue beads in her tiny hands sparkle as the sun hits the different facets, sending beams radiating from her hands onto the shaft of the great cross. As Josephine begins the second 'Hail Mary,' Maeve thinks on her own prayers like she did at Mass.

God, thank you so much for letting my daddy call me at Mass. I knew you heard me. I know you can help me. I'm glad you and I are friends. You can tell me if you need me to do something for you. I hope you are happy. And if you can, please help me get my hat back from the leprechaun. Amen.

Maeve moves her fingers to the third bead in the 'Hail Mary' line as she hears Auntie Jo begin the next prayer. She leans over and nudges Auntie Jo. Auntie Jo gives the high sign back without missing a beat.

With the third 'Hail Mary' said, Auntie Jo finishes with a 'Glory Be.' They both bless themselves.

"Now, that was very well done, Maeve. Ye kept tally like a pro. Shall we find a spot over there and enjoy our meal?"

"I am *really* hungry."

"To be sure. That was quite a hike, no matter the age."

Auntie Jo sees a perfect outcropping of rocks to sit on and view the amazing scenery stretched out before them. She pulls out the sandwiches and hands one to Maeve.

"Let's thank the Lord for these lovely sandwiches." Auntie Jo blesses herself, as does Maeve. "Thank ye Jesus, Mary, and Joseph for this food to eat. Please bless it and us. Amen. Now, dig in."

Maeve smells the sweet, pungent odor of the cheese poking out between the slices of thick, crusty bread. "This doesn't look like the bread my mom makes sandwiches with."

"It doesn't? Well, it's edible. Give it a bite."

Maeve slowly sinks her mish-mash of teeth into the foreign textures. Her eyebrows rise as the creamy taste of cheese hits her tongue.

"Wow, this is really good! I've never liked cheese sandwiches that much before."

"I'm glad ye like this one."

"All of that praying we've been doing must have made God really happy, that's why he made this sandwich taste better than even peanut butter and jelly!"

Auntie Jo smiles down at the ravenous little waif.

"Maeve, I want to remind ye of somethin' regardin' yer prayers now and this morning."

Maeve stops eating. "What's that?"

"Well, ye know when God answered yer prayer so fast today when yer daddy called?"

"Yes."

"Ye must realize 'tis not always the case that God responds so quickly. Don't be discouraged when yer prayers aren't answered as fast next time, or even at all the way ye want. Sometimes what we want is not what we need. God knows the difference, and what we want doesn't always happen."

"Why wouldn't God want what we want? Doesn't he want us to be happy?"

"His greatest aim is for us to be happy but what we want and what we need are not always the same. If God were to step in and make everythin' perfect all the time, we'd never learn anythin'. We'd be utterly miserable. We might as well be this rock we're sitting on. We'd never be tested and know how to use our free will for good. We'd never know how blessed we truly are."

Maeve stares off, considering this.

"When my son, Declan, and my daughter, Claire, were killed in a car crash, God didn't make that happen, but He did decide not to intervene, not to let me heal them, not to save them in this world, but rather to save them fer eternal life in the next. Losin' them was awfully hard and very sudden for me, but it taught me not to blame God. I learned to trust in Him to get me through the pain and on to livin' life again."

"Weren't you mad that God didn't save them or let you help them?"

Auntie Jo takes a deep breath as she looks out further past the vista of Clonmel.

"At first I was mad, but my anger didn't last. Fer I knew the truth, the truth that God had to witness his own Son, Jesus, die under the most horrific of circumstances, all fer our sins. If God and the Blessed Virgin could lose Their precious child fer me, I knew I could endure any loss put in my path. I know I'll see my dearies all again in a lovelier place with no pain or sufferin'." Auntie Jo stops to smile a moment before continuing.

"There are people who don't believe in any of this and see themselves smarter for their disbelief. I never needed the nuns to prove God, Jesus, or Mary was there fer me. It was in my fabric as a young child, well before the adults had uttered a word. I don't know if that had anything to do with my healin' abilities, but I took what I was given and did my best. All the awe and wonder I ever had was a direct reflection of my Creator. God has never been a riddle for me as He is for many folks. I suppose I'm either dumb or blessed, or both. The best part is that He's always teaching me somethin', no matter how old and crotchety I get."

"So, Jesus is different from God?"

Auntie Jo reaches down next to her and plucks a shamrock from the grass and passes it to Maeve.

"There is only one God, but three persons in that God. Sort of like how that is one shamrock but three leaves that make it up. All the leaves are equal and they are all part of one shamrock. God is three persons, God the Father, God the Son—who is Jesus—and God the Holy Ghost. All three make up our one God, which we call the Holy Trinity. Does that makes sense?"

"I think so." Maeve twirls the shamrock in her fingers.

"Whew, God is sure teaching ye a lot today!"

"Did God teach you anything today, Auntie Jo?"

"He certainly did. He taught me how lovely it is to be alive."

"But you already knew that."

"Not the way I know it now that I know ye."

Maeve beams, throwing her arms around a startled Auntie Jo.

"He taught me the same thing today too!"

Auntie Jo beams from ear to ear. "My goodness, we are twins, hah!"

Auntie Jo pulls out the chocolate éclairs from the lunch box. "Are ye ready for yer chocolate éclair?

"Yes ma'am!"

Auntie Jo holds both side by side. "Now which one would ye like?"

Maeve studies them for overall size and volume of chocolate coating. With chocolate being the determining factor, she points to the one on the right.

"Oooh, I knew ye'd pick that one. Fine choice."

Auntie Jo hands the chocolate pastry to Maeve who takes a big, slow bite.

After several chews, Maeve looks to Auntie Jo. "You should eat yours."

"I think I will."

Auntie Jo raises the luscious pastry to her mouth. The shoddy assembly of teeth do their best to tear through the flaky layers and custard. Maeve giggles as a huge blob of cream squirts out through a space in Auntie Jo's teeth and onto her chin. Snorts and chuckles erupt at the silliness of the sight.

"Kehoe's has some fine baked goods, but I'll have to tell them to go a bit easier on the custard!"

As Maeve munches on her éclair, Josephine asks, "So ye didn't mind going to church?"

"I thought it was good. I'm not even scared of Jesus and all that blood anymore."

"I know Jesus is happy to hear that."

"My favorite is Mary, though. She is so pretty, and she always smiles at me." Maeve looks up at Josephine. "I think you look like Mary."

"Oh, go on! This old woman's face? St. Mary forgive her, she's not serious!" Auntie Jo presses her hands together and looks towards the sky.

"You do, especially your eyes. They sparkle like Mary's."

Josephine hugs the little girl tight as her sparkly eyes moisten with tears. "Ye are a sweet one, that ye are. Now, it's time we head back down. We need to pick up somethin' to eat this evening. What does yer mother like?"

"Her favorite sandwich is a BLT."

"What in good heaven's is a BLT?"

"Bacon, lettuce and tomato, but she likes cheese on hers too, melted."

"Ah, melted. Sounds delicious. Well, let's see if we can get the makin's fer such a feast."

Auntie Jo and Maeve clasp hands and start down the rocky dirt path.

"Can we come back here again?" Maeve asks.

"If my bones cooperate, I would think so."

Two lambs run in front of Maeve and Auntie Jo, kicking their back hooves up and jumping about.

"Look at the wee ones playin', what fun it is they're havin' together!"

Maeve wants to chase after the little lambs and play in the field with them. Instead, she stays by her friend's side, knowing that though Auntie Jo is walking well, she cannot run and play.

CHAPTER 16

OLD POTATO

The butcher hands Josephine an inch stack of meat. "Ere's yer bacon, Josephine."

Maeve tugs on Josephine's sleeve, "That doesn't look like bacon, Auntie Jo."

"It doesn't?"

They both examine the pork.

"Ah, American bacon is different than our rashers, isn't it? Well, with the melted cheese she'll not notice. Ya think?"

Maeve shrugs.

"What hour is it, Maeve, let me see?' Josephine checks her watch. "We've time for a quick set on the high stool. Let's pay fer the groceries and we'll be off to Whelan's."

"What's the high stool?"

"The seats in the pub at the bar where the people go for a drink and to tell a tale or two."

They pay the cashier and hit the street, heading up town for Whelan's. After a five-minute walk, Maeve and Josephine enter the dim lighting of Whelan's Undertaker and Bar. Maeve climbs up on one of the high stools and rests both elbows on the shiny oak bar. The barkeep, Fergus, meets Josephine and Maeve with a smile brighter than any of the bar's bulbs.

"Two days in a row, Josephine! Are ye going fer some sort of Guinness Record is it?

"No Fergus, Smithwicks please, not Guinness."

"Smithwicks it is, and fer the wee one?"

Josephine turns to Maeve. "Maeve, would ye like a cola, or maybe a lemonade?"

"Lemonade, please."

"So polite, she is. This is yer grandniece, is it?"

"Maeve, she's my great-grand."

"And she's the head of ye, Josephine."

Josephine and Maeve roll their eyes at each other over the reoccurring comparison.

"She favors me a bit in the eyes, I suppose." Josephine winks to Maeve. Maeve answers with a wink that's more of a blink.

Fergus sets off to get their drinks as Immaculata McClure enters the pub. "Ah, it's the twins! How are ye girls? Did ye see the fairies?"

Fergus serves Maeve her lemonade along with a plate of fries.

"No, we walked by the covered wood but, would ye believe, Maeve would have none of goin' inside."

"I don't blame ye, Maeve. I never fancied that covered wood. Yer great granny and Josephine nearly lived in there when we were young. They were the bold ones."

Maeve purses her lips deep in thought. "Does everyone in Ireland believe in fairies? I don't think people in America do."

Fergus chimes in from behind the bar. "I don't know about everyone, but belief in the little people is still alive and well. Farmers all over Ireland have left ring forts on their land untouched for hundreds of years fer fear of makin' the fairies mad and bringin' misfortune their way."

Maeve takes a swig of her lemonade. "Auntie Jo, this isn't lemonade."

"It isn't? Let me taste."

Josephine takes a swig. "Sure, it is. Ye don't like it?"

"It tastes kind of like 7-Up, not like lemonade in America. But it's good. Can I have some ketchup for my fries?"

"Ketchup? Fries? Ah, ye mean red sauce for yer chips. Fergus, have ye some red sauce for the chips?"

Fergus nods and goes to fetch some.

Josephine turns the conversation back to Immaculata. "I seem to remember one Immaculata Ryan bein' the girl who stole the Tinker woman's broom! Nothing I ever did compared to the boldness of *that* act."

Josephine takes a sip of her Smithwicks.

"Except perhaps kissin' someone else's husband."

Josephine about chokes on her mouthful of Smithwicks while Immaculata begins laughing with delight.

"Caught ye off guard with that one, did I, Jo?"

"Immaculata! How long have ye known? Ye know it meant nothin'."

"Calm yerself, Jo. Denis told me the moment I got home from my mother's. He was racked with guilt and couldn't bear to look me in the eye, till he told me the sordid details."

"Oh heavens, what ye must have thought of me all these years?"

"I thought nothin' ill of ye. I knew ye loved only Teddy and it was Denis who kissed ye out of drink. He was ever the flirt and the rascal. I knew that before I ever married him, but he was true to a fault. I'm just razzin' ya, Jo."

"But to think Denis told ye… and I never came clean to Teddy. I'll be in purgatory a good long while over this one."

"Oh, yer talkin' crazy. Any woman worth her salt keeps a gentle secret or two from her husband! Think of it: had ye told Teddy, his and Denis' friendship would never have survived. Ye knew it meant nothin'. Ye did the right thing."

"I suppose yer right, Mackie, it's the hush-hush that keeps the mystery about a woman."

Immaculata raises her glass. "Of course 'tis, now let's have another. Fergus!"

At that moment, Micheleen walks in to the pub. It takes a good moment to let her eyes adjust to the less than illuminated conditions. Finally, she recognizes Maeve and Josephine sitting next to Immaculata at the bar.

"Auntie Jo?"

The three women of intrigue turn to greet Micheleen.

"Ah, Micheleen! Ye found us! Did every person on the street tell ye we were here?"

"Don't plan on robbing a bank anytime soon! I was directed here without me even asking."

Josephine raises her glass. "That's Ireland, few secrets last long here." She winks at Immaculata.

"Mommy!" Maeve leaps from the high stool and gives her mom a huge hug. "Daddy's coming to visit us here in Ireland!"

The color drains from Micheleen's face. "Wh- What are you talking about?"

"Trust me, if he does actually get on a plane to come here, it's just to see Maeve. We have nothing in common anymore. He's bored with my ambitions and career and I'm bored with… well…with him."

"Seems ye two have something in common…yer both bored. Sounds like a perfect pair to me!" Josephine needlessly waits for Micheleen to smile at the joke.

Immaculata sits up straight. "Bored? Are ye serious, Micheleen? Ye know, boredom is a reflection of yer own mind. It's more to do with who ye are than whom yer with. And where in the marriage vows does it say love, honor, and keep the excitement comin' at all times of the day and night, till death do ye part?"

"Actually, we never said any vows, but that's beside the point. We were both too young, and now we agree that separate living is best."

Josephine takes a turn. "Dearie, I know ye think you've thought this through, but this affects more than ye and… what's his name?"

"James."

"James, right. What a nice name that is. I've always liked that name."

"We *have* thought this through. Maeve is better off living with happy parents who are apart than with miserable parents who are together."

Immaculata looks Micheleen up and down. "And this is ye being happy?"

"I'm just jet-lagged. Believe me, I'll be much happier here. We've tried to work through our issues. We went to counseling and everything. We're just not soul mates."

"Soul mates? What the divil?" bursts out Immaculata. "Ye get married takin' no vows and yer concerned with being soul mates? Dearie, no wonder yer marriage failed, ye went at it arse backwards. Seems to me ye need to work on yer own soul before lookin' for someone else's."

"Immaculata! Stop flapping yer tongue. Pay her no mind, Micheleen. Only ye and James know what went on between ye. One thing's certain, ye made quite a lovely child."

Josephine glances over at Maeve and smiles.

"Oh, please Jo, could ye pat yerself on the back any harder, with her being yer identical twin and all?"

Josephine shrugs while Micheleen tilts her head back to polish off her drink.

Immaculata motions to Fergus to get Micheleen another.

Josephine isn't convinced she's getting the full story. "Micheleen, are ye sure there wasn't more to breakin' up than boredom? Was there... another woman?"

Micheleen chuckles as she sips. "No! Definitely not. James is...well, if you knew James, you'd know he's all about practicing medicine. I told you, he is boring. His career is literally all he thinks about. He's very kind, but he's as exciting as...as...an old potato."

"A potato can be exciting if ye know how to cook it." Josephine quips.

"Auntie Jo!"

Immaculata leans forward. "She's right Micheleen. Old potatoes can be hot potatoes if ye use the right recipe."

"The only kind of potato James can be is bland and boiled. And besides, I'm on a no-carb diet."

Josephine finishes her Smithwicks.

"Suit yerself, but I warn ye, with a bit of salt and butter, boiled potatoes are a popular dish. Ye just may find yerself craving carbs again. And ye better be careful because before ye know it yer boiled potato will be on someone else's plate."

Micheleen takes a sip of her second vodka martini.

"Isn't vodka made from potatoes?" Immaculata quips.

Micheleen spews her mouthful back into her glass and waves down Fergus.

"Fergus, I'll take a tequila tonic with a spritz of lime."

Micheleen turns to Immaculata. "It's time for a little excitement."

CHAPTER 17

TWO RIDDLED SHOES

Josephine opens the cottage door. Maeve races in past her with Micheleen slowly following.

"Why don't ye go lie down for a spell, Micheleen? Maeve and I will call ye when the BLTs are ready."

"I will definitely take you up on that offer. I'm exhausted." Micheleen yawns and heads to the bedroom.

"Maeve, be sure to help Auntie Jo with whatever she needs!" She yells as she closes the door.

Micheleen pulls back the flowered comforter and climbs into the sheets without changing out of her work clothes. As she flops her head on the down pillow, she feels something hard underneath. She sits back up and lifts the pillow, revealing a little black shoe.

"Why in the world would Maeve put that lost toddler shoe under my pillow?"

Too tired to consider the possible motivations, she puts the shoe on the nightstand and quickly drifts off to sleep.

In the kitchen Maeve helps Auntie Jo ready the sandwiches.

"Go ahead and put the bread in the toaster Dearie, if ye don't mind."

Maeve places two slices in the electric toaster and pushes the button down. She peers inside, watching the electric coils turn from black to red. The heat wafts up and kisses her cheeks. The smell of the Irish rashers cooking lures Maeve's nose and eyes toward the crackling action. As the lovely scent tickles her nostrils, she observes the white-haired chef by her side.

Auntie Jo catches Maeve looking at her and flashes her toothless grin. Maeve beams back with her own toothy smile.

Maeve wiggles her tongue across the hole in her mouth and crosses something sharp. Soon she and Auntie Jo will not be quite as identical as they are right now.

"Pooh!"

"What's the matter, Darlin'?"

"My tooth is coming in. Our smiles aren't going to match for long."

"Oh, but they will. Ye and I have the same sense of humor, and as long as one of us smiles, the other will too. That's the matching that counts."

Auntie Jo gives Maeve a wink. Maeve answers her with an attempted wink-blink.

"Auntie Jo, where are we going tomorrow?"

"Did ye enjoy yerself today, did ya?"

"I had so much fun! I can't wait to tell Mommy more about what we did!"

"Did ye miss yer video game?"

"Nope."

Maeve had forgotten about the video game that had been her fifth appendage until this morning. The live action that she and Auntie Jo experienced today far outweighed the entertainment value provided in a little video screen. Curious as to where the game is all the same, Maeve scans the kitchen but does not see the once invaluable device.

"Auntie Jo, do you know where it is?"

"Last I saw it was this mornin', here on the kitchen counter. Did ye take it back to ye room?"

Maeve runs into her room, eyeing the Jesus for the first time since last night. She thinks how silly she was to be scared of him. She looks around her bed, on the dresser, and scours the vanity, barely even taking note of the brand-new laptop next to the statue of the Blessed Virgin.

Maeve tiptoes into her mother's room and looks around in there. The little black shoe on the nightstand catches her eye. It looks just like the one she found yesterday. Maeve picks it up and rushes to show Auntie Jo.

Micheleen stirs, but only for a moment before returning to her slumber.

"Auntie Jo!"

"What 'tis it, darlin'?"

"It's another one. I found it on the table in Mommy's room!" She holds the shoe out to Auntie Jo who takes it and looks it over top to bottom. Maeve retrieves the first one from Josephine's purse and gives it to Josephine to compare.

"That divil. Did ye find yer video game?" Maeve shakes her head in the negative. "Guess ye can stop lookin' fer it then. He's taken it and left ye another lovely right shoe. Heh, heh, heh."

"I thought you said leprechauns don't like things like video games?"

"They don't, unless they can have them fer themselves. I never said leprechauns weren't hypocrites."

She looks back at the shoes, "What fine work they are, all hand stitched and gorgeous. Ye must take good care of these. Keep them together, or else he'll steal them back and ye'll be all out of luck. The magic is in the pair."

"Why did he leave another right shoe? Why not a left one?"

"Tis a sign of some sort, two right shoes. Sure, I'd take it as good, since right shoes are lucky, but there's a riddle in there somewhere. The leprechauns are famous fer riddles. Solve it and yer due a wish fer sure."

Micheleen walks into the hubbub. "Whatever you're cooking smells so wonderful it woke me up, Auntie Jo."

"I'm sorry, dearie. I told ye we were makin' yer BLTs."

Micheleen sees the meat in the pan. "Irish BLTs, I see. Yum! I thought I would sleep but my stomach is telling me I'm more hungry than tired."

She spies the two little black shoes lying on the chair. "Wait a minute. You have two now?"

Micheleen picks them up together. "Two right shoes? How do you make a pair out of two right shoes?"

"That's it! That's the riddle the leprechaun wants us to figure out! Good going, Micheleen. Maeve, get yer thinkin' cap on."

"Leprechaun?"

"Yes, Mommy, he took my hat and my tablet and left us these shoes. That's what leprechauns do. If I can figure out the riddle, I'll get a wish!" Maeve jumps up and down.

"I'd wish for your stuff back, because these aren't going to do you much good."

"Oh Micheleen, ye have little faith. Maeve's due fer a wish if she can solve the riddle."

Maeve jumps in. "It's okay, Auntie Jo, I have enough faith for the both of us." Maeve smiles.

"Mommy, Auntie Jo showed me how to pray today in Mass ,and when I did, Daddy called on your phone right when I asked God to let me talk to him! Auntie Jo said it was a miracle, just like her bones." The words are tumbling out of Maeve's mouth faster than she can enunciate. "God doesn't always answer prayers like that, but everyone should pray every day anyway. God has been working as hard as you have today, I bet."

Maeve's mother hugs her, "A bit more than me, I'd say. I'm glad Auntie Jo is teaching you about God. I'm afraid that's a topic I'm not very familiar with."

"We also went up to the Holy Spot and she told me about the leprechauns and fairies. There's a big difference you know."

Micheleen smiles, "Reminds me of my dad telling me about Irish folklore. I loved those stories! Don't tell your father, though. He's not one for fairytales."

Maeve continues, "Well, I today learned how fries are called chips, and how bacon and lemonade are different here in Ireland, and that Auntie Jo kissed Immaculata's husband."

"Woah, Maeve! Slow down. Yer talkin' yer mother's ear off."

Josephine pats Maeve on the head and then looks to Micheleen. "Oh, she's a parrot, that one is. It was a joke about Immaculata's husband, Maeve. We were just jokin'."

Auntie Jo starts placing the steaming rashers on a plate.

"Well, I have no idea how long the pain in my bones will stay away, so we've got to do all we can, while we can. Maeve! The toast!"

Maeve rushes over and attempts to retrieve the charred slices of bread. Auntie Jo unplugs the toaster and helps her unwedge the burned pieces.

"This slice here must have gotten stuck and didn't let them pop up. It happens sometimes. We'll try it again, but this time, Maeve, ye must watch. Once they get golden, tell me and I'll unplug it so we can catch them before they burn."

Plugging the toaster back in, Maeve goes for a second try at the toast. Auntie Jo wipes up the black crumbs.

Maeve keeps watch while getting down to what has been in the back of her mind all day. "Mommy, when are you calling Daddy back to find out when he's coming?"

Micheleen sits at the kitchen table, sighs, then exhales deeply. "I'll call him later Maeve; I need to eat something first."

"I hope he can stay a really long time. I want to take Daddy to all the places we went today."

"Your father, in a church? That would be something to see." Micheleen huffs.

Josephine looks past Micheleen's tough exterior and examines the hurting woman in front of her. She sits beside her at the table.

"James is not a religious man?"

"No. He was actually baptized Catholic, but now he thinks religion is corrupt mind control, as he puts it."

"Scared of the sacred, is he? Sounds like he's a need-to-knower not a need-to-believer."

"Belief in God is the same as fairytales to him."

"Ye mentioned he practices medicine?"

"Yes, he's a doctor."

"Hmmm. No faith healer is he." Josephine is struck by this information and rubs her chin.

"A doctor? What sort of doctor?"

"He's an internist, best in his field…or so they say."

Josephine can sense she's getting close to the heart wound. "Maeve, how's the toast?"

"It's ready."

Josephine hops up and unplugs the toaster, removing two perfectly golden-brown slices. "Lovely, I'll make the first for yer mam. Oh, but look, I've forgotten to get the mayonnaise out of the storage hut in the yard. Maeve, dearie, please go out and get me a jar of mayonnaise."

Maeve looks to Josephine in horror. "What about the owl?"

"Maeve, the owl will not come near ye again."

"But…"

"That's a challenge God has given ye, now go. Pray for His protection."

Maeve slowly walks out the cottage back door and crosses herself.

Josephine turns back to Micheleen as she feigns surprise at finding a jar of mayonnaise already in the cupboard.

"Oh, lookie here. Oh, well, it never hurts to have a spare."

She assembles the Irish BLT while continuing the line of questions.

"So, James is an internist? Did he tend to yer parents durin' their illnesses?"

Micheleen looks down at her hands resting on the table and twiddles her thumbs. "No, not directly."

"But he should have saved them, is that it?"

"No. I never said that."

"But you thought it, didn't ye? Micheleen, I know yer hurtin' after losin' yer mah and dah, but that was not James' fault. No matter how great a doctor…"

"Auntie Jo, I don't mean to interrupt, but my problem with James has nothing to do with my parents."

Josephine stands still, studying Micheleen.

Micheleen continues, "Well…at least it has nothing to do with his abilities as a doctor."

"Then why are ye blamin' him?"

"I'm not! For that, I'm not."

Josephine takes a moment to pray for some guidance. "Then why do ye hang your mournin' on yer marriage?"

Micheleen gives Josephine the side-eye. "Who said that's what I'm doing?"

"Micheleen, the marriage died with your father, this I know."

Micheleen shifts her weight in her chair. "Maybe so…but it had nothing to do with James not saving my parents."

"Then what was it, dearie?"

Tears begin to form in Micheleen's eyes.

"He didn't care. He didn't feel anything at the end of their lives, no emotion at all! To him their passing was like reading an article in the newspaper. He didn't even let me pray."

Josephine gets up to fetch Micheleen a tissue.

"What do ye mean he didn't let ye pray?"

"The night Dad passed, I knelt next to his bed and prayed. I didn't know what I was doing, I just knew I needed to do it, and that he needed me to. James walked in on me and showed nothing but-but disbelief, disgust. He asked me what I was doing. When I told him I was praying he said, 'Why? It's not going to change anything. He is dying.'"

Micheleen wipes her wet face and clears her throat. "Even though we were in the same house, it felt like we were oceans apart. After that, it ended. I just couldn't bring myself to love him anymore."

Josephine embraces a sobbing Micheleen.

"It's okay, darlin', it's all goin' to be okay. Here, eat your sandwich." She places the assemblage before Micheleen.

"This looks delicious. Thank you." Micheleen wipes her tears and tries to dry her face.

Maeve whips through the front door and slams it loudly, exhaling slow and low on the other side.

Micheleen and Auntie Jo both turn toward Maeve, the mayonnaise jar clutched in hand bobbing up and down against her chest with each heavy breath.

"Got it, Auntie Jo!"

"Brilliant, Maeve. I found another jar here behind a can of beans, but I'll need yer jar eventually too. Thank ye, darlin'."

Maeve cannot believe she just risked blood and scalp again, all for an unnecessary jar of mayonnaise, but the look on her mother's face tells her not to make a big deal out of it.

"Are you okay, Mommy?

Her mother raises the sandwich, "I'm fine, just starving."

Before she can take her first bite Maeve yells, "Wait Mommy! Thank God for your food!"

Micheleen puts the sandwich down gently. "You're right, can you show me?"

Maeve begins as Micheleen and Auntie Jo follow. "In the name of the Father, and of the Son, and of the Holy Ghost. Amen. Jesus, Mary, and Joseph, thank you for this delicious food. Please bless it and us. Amen."

All three make another Sign of the Cross.

Micheleen smiles, "That was lovely, Maeve."

"Well done, Maeve, well done. We'll learn the longer blessin' of the food later. God has His ears full today from ye, and I know He's smilin' at hearin' yer voice each time."

As Micheleen takes her first bite of the toasted delicacy, Maeve pleads, "Mommy, will you call Daddy now?"

"Maeve, leave yer mam be. Mind that toast, don't let it burn."

Maeve returns her attention to the toast, signaling its readiness. Auntie Jo unplugs as Maeve pulls the slices out.

"I like making toast with you, Auntie Jo."

"I like it too, darlin'."

CHAPTER 18

hell phones

Josephine's eyes open to her sunlit room. She lies still, waiting for the expected twinge of pain. With no pulsing ache, she continues her morning ritual, moving her legs over to the side of the bed.

Still not yet out of breath, she reaches for the bedpost. Stiffness grips her joints, but pain is not keeping her from raising herself swiftly. Josephine says a quick prayer of thanks to God for her continued mobility.

Josephine's knees seem the weakest of her joints, as stepping down each stair sends a shooting pain up her legs, but it's nothing she hasn't walked through before. With the stairs tackled, the stride down the hall is a walk in the park. She makes her way to the kitchen to start making Maeve breakfast.

Josephine spies an open package of Hob Nob biscuits, surmising it was Micheleen's morning meal. Josephine brushes the crumbs into her hand, opening the back door and flinging the morsels outside for the birds to clean up.

With the remaining rashers in the pan cooking, Josephine goes to check on a still-sleeping Maeve. She sits gently on the edge of Maeve's bed and lightly strokes her head to wake her softly. Maeve opens her eyes.

"Tis better than the way I woke ye yesterday, tisn't it?"

"Your bones don't hurt?"

"Not too bad. Get yerself dressed and come eat some breakfast. We'll go to Patrick's Well and then on to Mass before we head to Michelstown Caves." Josephine gets up.

"Should we bring the shoes with us?"

"We should keep them with us till ye solve the riddle. Give 'em to me and I'll put 'em in my bag with the mobile yer mother wants with us."

Maeve passes the little black shoes over to Josephine. "Mommy loves cell phones."

"Hell phones if ye ask me."

"Hell phones. That's funny." Maeve chuckles.

"Yer not to repeat such words, Maeve." Josephine wags her index finger in Maeve's direction.

"What words?" Maeve tries to wink.

Josephine winks back. "Exactly. Now go get dressed."

Josephine opens the iron gate to Patrick's Well, letting Maeve walk in past her. Maeve stands frozen at the sight of it. "Is this place magic?"

"No, dearie, not magic. It's holy, very holy. Come now, walk carefully down the steps. They can be a bit slick with the mornin' dew."

The two make their way down the rough slab stairs to the stone-encrusted lake. At the center of the peaceful pool, on a small rock-laden island, stands a carved Celtic cross. Although it is weathered by time, it is decidedly clear as to its meaning after all these centuries.

"Maeve, this place was long ago considered a sacred spot to the ancient Celts. The Celts were pagans and worshiped many gods. They'd bring gifts to this well in offerin's to the goddess they believed lived at the bottom of the spring. The poorest of folks used to bring rags as their offerin's, for that was all they had. They would tie the rags to these very trees growin' by this sacred well. Even before they were Catholics, the people knew the mystical properties held in these waters."

Josephine and Maeve tread over the small stone bridge near the source of the spring.

"When St. Patrick came to Ireland, he told the pagans they were right about the well bein' sacred, but it was God the Father whose power and holiness was at work here. Upon teachin' the people this, Patrick baptized the pagans in the waters, makin' them the first Catholics of Ireland. They placed the cross in the center there, and from that point on called this Patrick's Well. It is a sure thing yer very own ancestors were baptized here by the great saint himself. And to think the seeds of faith he planted long ago are still bearin' fruit here and around the globe."

Maeve stands in awe. "Cool! Can we stay here all day?"

"Oh no, dearie. I just wanted ye to see the spot and get some of the holy water fer yerself. We must be goin' soon, in order to make it to Mass on time. We'll come back later when we're not in a rush."

Josephine pulls a little glass bottle out of her purse. "Here, now fill it with water so ye'll have some of yer own."

Maeve dips the bottle in the sacred liquid, watching the bottle go from empty to full. "Do I drink it?"

"Ye can have a sip now."

Maeve takes a swig. "That's good."

"We'll get some to have at home to use for blessin' whenever ye want."

"Cool."

Maeve screws the top on the bottle tightly and hands it back to Josephine to be placed in her satchel of all things important. Josephine takes her rosary out of the bag and quickly dips it in the holy pool.

"Even a rosary likes a bath now and then. Off we go. Father Adrian won't keep Mass on hold just fer us."

"Doesn't he know our ancestors knew St. Patrick?"

"All the more reason we shouldn't be late fer Mass. Catholic guilt by association, don'tcha know?"

With a Sign of the Cross, the two leave the sacred waters.

CHAPTER 19

Deli Bread

Josephine and Maeve enter through the doors of the Friary just as they had the day before. The same cast of characters is seen sitting in the same seats, as if they haven't left.

"Auntie Jo, why is everyone in the same places as yesterday?"

"People from the West end of town all sit on the right side, whereas the Irishtown folks all sit on the left. It's been that way since I was a girl. No written rule, just the way 'tis."

"Can't they sit closer if they want?"

"They can, but they don't want to. Sometimes havin' a routine is the biggest freedom of all."

Maeve follows Josephine around to each of the statues, saying their prayers until they revisit their pew from yesterday. Josephine continues to pray as Maeve sits back and admires the decorative architecture covering every inch of the ancient building. Hand-carved faces of saints and benefactors of the past adorn the arches and lintels crisscrossing the ceiling.

Father Adrian enters from the right side of the altar. Maeve sees a smile break across Auntie Jo's face. Auntie Jo makes the Sign of the Cross at the sight of the friar. Maeve tugs on Auntie Jo's sleeve, "Can I use your rosary beads?"

Auntie Jo tries to fish them out of her overcrowded bag. She feels around the leprechaun shoes, the cell phone, wrapped sandwiches, her wallet, a handkerchief, and the bottle of Patrick's Well water, finding no beads.

"Where the divil are they? They had a dip at the well." She feels some more. "Ah, here darlin'." She hands the blue crystal beads to Maeve.

Maeve kneels and says a seven-year-old's version of the "Our Father," asking God to "give us today our Deli bread."

Josephine chuckles, "Oh no, Maeve, it's our *daily* bread we ask for."

"Okay." Maeve continues, forgiving those who "miss Mass against us" and "deliver us some evil."

Josephine corrects, "*From* evil, Darlin."

"From evil, Amen."

Father Adrian begins Mass; the assorted elderly die-hards and little Maeve are the only ones in attendance. As the Mass proceeds, two or three others dribble in. Maeve continues to pray the rosary as best as she can until it is time to go up for Communion.

Father Adrian puts the Holy Eucharist on Josephine's tongue then blesses the forehead of little Maeve. They return to their pew and kneel just as the "hell phone" in Josephine's purse chimes out the tune *Some Enchanted Evening*.

"Oh, fer the love of Pete!"

Josephine scrambles through the satchel to find the chiming menace. She pulls out one of the leprechaun shoes to better find and silence the source. Father Adrian pauses while Josephine tries to locate the device. Much like the day before, the other patrons glare at Josephine and Maeve while the tune continues to ping out in high-pitched tones. Father Adrian smiles as Josephine hands the phone off to Maeve like a hot potato.

"Quick Maeve, answer it."

"Hello? Daddy! Praying worked again!" Maeve looks to Josephine in utter amazement.

In a hushed voice, Josephine hustles her out.

"Maeve, get up. Go outside, go."

The two of them make a beeline to the friary doors and exit, letting the great doors slam behind them.

Father Adrian chuckles while the rest of his stone-faced congregation stare back at him. He regains his composure and says the closing words of the Mass.

Outside, Maeve ends her conversation with her father. "I can't wait to see you tomorrow, Daddy. I love you too. Bye!" Maeve punches the 'end call' button.

"For someone who doesn't go to church, yer father certainly doesn't mind phonin' his prayers in! How'd he get that cell number?"

"I gave it to him last night when Mommy let me call him."

"So, he'll be here tomorrow?"

"Yes! I'm sooooo excited!"

"At least we know we won't be gettin' a call from him then! My goodness! Two days in a row."

Others begin filing out of church, scowling at Josephine and Maeve as they walk past. Father Adrian is the last to exit. He strolls over to the disruptive duo.

"I see ye've gone hi-tech, Josephine?"

"I'm so sorry, Father. I forgot to turn the cruel thing off."

"Not to worry, I've been known to disrupt some solemn occasions myself, lately. It happens. I hope the call wasn't serious?"

"It was Maeve's father. He'll be here tomorrow fer a visit."

"Visit?" Father Adrian looks to Maeve. "Will he not be stayin' on with ye?"

Josephine motions over Maeve's head to Father Adrian with her fingers in a splitting motion as she mouths to him, "The parents are separated."

"I've been praying Daddy will stay. So far, God has listened to what I want."

Father Adrian kneels to Maeve's level. "Maeve, God always listens. Though sometimes things turn out to be a way that ye and I don't like or understand at first. But in the end, we will see why and know God loves us above all else."

"I know. It's still fun to talk to Him, even if things don't go how I want them to."

"Yes, it certainly is. I wish everyone knew our secret."

Father Adrian pats Maeve on the top of the head as he stands back up slowly. Josephine takes note of the priest's careful movement.

"Ye certainly look better than ye did yesterday, Father, but I still see a bit of hesitation in yer movement."

"I feel better. And yerself?"

"Father, I was 20 years younger yesterday. Maeve and I climbed all the way to the Holy Spot, but even so, I still couldn't go through the covered fairy wood with its steep slope and low ceilin'. My stiffness is back today, but the pain is manageable. I figure I better use my bones while I can, so we're headed to Michelstown Caves where we hope to spy the fairies. I should be able to manage the caves, a much more forgivin' walk than the covered wood."

"Josephine, ye should know better than to fill the child's head with fairy nonsense."

"Ah, but Father, ye know as well as I: God made the enchanted just as he made us. We're not goin' to join their ranks, just out to see them like the birdwatcher observes a bird. Shame on ye. Being an Irishman, ye should have more respect fer the less than human amongst us."

"Ye sound like my sainted mutter. Never a holier woman I knew, but her talk of the fairies was with her to her last day."

"Wise woman."

"Is there any other kind?"

"Which makes ye a wise man."

Josephine takes Maeve's hand and begins to turn down the street. "Good day, Father."

Father Adrian turns to reenter the friary.

"Oh, and Father?"

"Yes, Josephine."

"Thank ye for lettin' me climb up to the Holy Spot yesterday."

"That wasn't me."

"It was the He in ye."

Father Adrian smiles and waves to Josephine.

"Well, ye two have a brilliant time today. Give my regards to the fairies." He chuckles and shakes his head as he strolls into the friary.

CHAPTER 20

ROAD TO MICHELSTOWN CAVES

The pair make their way up through town, crossing over to the Cahir Road. The sky sparkles clear as a day can. The breeze is at their backs, which Josephine takes to be a good sign. As the twosome cross over to the east side of the road, a little roller-skate of a car pulls up next to them and slows.

Fergus rolls down his window, "Where are ye ladies headed? Can I give you a lift?"

"We're on our way to Michelstown. Maeve wants to see the caves."

"Michelstown?! Josephine, have ye gone addled? You couldn't make it there and back before nightfall on shank's mare!"

"I've done it many times, Fergus. There's no need for dramatics."

"Get in, ye hard-headed woman." Fergus reaches over and

opens the passenger side. Maeve squeezes in the back as Josephine plops down in the front.

Fergus raises his eyebrows at Josephine. "Could ye slide a bit closer to yer own door, please?"

"What are ye talking about?"

"Knowing yer past, I just want to make sure ye don't try to steal a kiss while I'm trying to drive."

"Fergus, ye've none to worry. My charitable days are over."

With a belly laugh, Fergus throws the car in gear and puts pedal to metal. All three heads in the little sardine can snap back as they race on to Michelstown. Maeve looks out the window at the green blur of Irish countryside.

Fergus slows down and turns onto a narrower country road.

"Fergus, are ye daft? Michelstown is the other direction."

"I know. I'm swinging by Simon Carroll's in Fethard first. We're low on make-up and Kevin has a body comin' in this afternoon to make ready fer a Saturday burial."

"Who is it?"

"Seamus Dunne."

"Of the Carrick Dunnes?"

"Very same."

"And tight Simon Carroll's willin' to lend ye mortician make-up? I always pegged him fer a mean divil."

"Oh, he is. Make no mistake. He's not lendin' us a thing out of kindness. He lost a huge wager on a horse and owes Kevin's brother, the Bookmaker. The cosmetics are a tiny percentage of his debt. If he doesn't come up with the funds by week's end, I may very well be working at two undertaker and bar establishments!"

"Cornerin' the market on bodies and sotties."

"Recession proof on top of it!" Fergus slams on the breaks in front of Simon Carroll's, snapping everyone's head back, as is his custom.

"I'll be but a minute."

Fergus hops out and jogs inside the cheerfully painted building.

Maeve admires the multitude of hues. "This building is painted really pretty, sort of like the inside of your house."

"No lack for vibrancy to be sure. Colors placed properly, not an evil spirit can venture near."

"Are there dead people in this place, like where Fergus works?"

"I would say so."

"I don't think we have places like that back home. I think they keep the dead people away from the living ones in America."

"That's a shame. The dead ones tend to be so much more polite."

As Fergus returns to the car, a cloudburst erupts over them out of nowhere, the clear blue sky still gleaming up ahead of them. Quickly, Fergus reaches into the driver's side and pulls the lever to pop the trunk. He loads the make-up in the boot and rushes back to the driver's side, dripping wet as he climbs back in.

"Ladies, ye may be takin' a chance goin' to the caves. That's the direction the clouds are rollin' in from."

"Do ye mind drivin' us over there anyway? I'm sure the rain will be past once we get there."

The rain only falls harder as the tiny car speeds its way towards the Michelstown Caves. The windshield wipers swoosh back and forth frantically with little effect. Fergus' vision is impaired, but he finds this no reason to slow down in the least. With a great splash, they ride through a sizeable hole in the road, spraying a wave of water in all directions and landing the buggy in a deep Irish ditch. Fergus attempts to accelerate out of it but only digs his wheels deeper into the mud.

"Oh, fer heaven's sake Fergus, now we're stuck."

Fergus exits the car. "Alert the BBC."

"Well, it's yer own fault, driving like a madman in a thrashin' rainstorm."

Fergus looks up to the wet heavens. "No good deed goes unpunished."

He examines the front and back tires and then returns with the verdict. "Ye two keep tight here. I'll go for help back in Fethard. I know Daniel Malone has a tractor that could pull us out."

"How long will ye be?"

"I'll be back after a pint or two."

Josephine rolls her eyes as she rolls up the window.

Fergus heads off in the direction they came. The rain is so heavy, his form disappears in the wall of water within steps.

Josephine turns to talk to Maeve in the rear seat. "Why don't ye climb up here and sit in the driver's seat? Fergus will be gone for quite a bit."

Maeve welcomes the chance to sit behind the wheel and pretend to drive. After tumbling her way to the front, she pulls herself up to see over the steering wheel as she maneuvers amidst imaginary obstacles on the road. Josephine watches the erratic movements of the small driver sitting to her right.

"I believe yer better at that than Fergus."

Maeve smiles at the compliment. "Do you think it's raining too hard to go to the caves?"

Josephine cranes her neck to see off in the distance but cannot see beyond the heavy rain. "Can't tell. Ye know, it's a fact ye can have all four seasons here in Ireland in one day. The weather blows in and over so fast, ye just can't tell. Now watch where yer drivin', ye almost hit that cow!"

Maeve giggles at Josephine's joking and begins steering madly.

Josephine grabs the dashboard. "Oh my heavens, is Fergus drivin' again?!"

They both laugh hard at Fergus' expense before Maeve returns to more sensible 'driving.'

"Auntie Jo, do you think my mommy and daddy will get married again?"

"I don't know, Maeve. That's between them and God."

"If I solve the shoe riddle, can I wish for that?"

"Ye could. But be forewarned, the leprechaun can only put them under enchantment. It wouldn't be the same as it bein' their own choice."

"Why not?"

"Well, the enchantment, no matter how powerful, always wears off eventually. It could last a day, a year, a hundred years."

"It's worth trying."

"Perhaps. But, as they say, be careful what ye wish for."

Maeve pretends to steer around a corner. "What would you wish for, Auntie Jo?"

"Hmmm, I'd wish for a chocolate éclair from Kehoe's Bakery."

"That's not a wish! You can get that any day."

"Not for free."

Maeve is not satisfied with Josephine's wish. "Why not wish that your bones never hurt again?"

"Pain or no pain, they're still old bones in an old body. I'd rather have the lovely éclair."

"You could wish to not be old."

"Dearie, I am an old woman and proud of it. 'Tis God's design. Our bodies grow old so we are more willing to leave worldly things behind and go back to where we belong—with our Creator. The important thing is God gives us souls that never grow old. Believe me, I'll not be old forever once I'm with God. Wishin' to go backwards isn't the way to get there. The best is yet to come."

Maeve continues, "But to be young again you have to die."

"Yes."

"I don't ever want to die."

Josephine looks at the diminutive driver and responds sagely, "Ah, but most of your heart will be up in heaven by the time you're old."

"How?"

"Because when you're old like me, most of your loved ones have gone to God, and a bit of your own heart goes with them each time. That's why it hurts when someone you love dies. 'Tis God's design."

"Why would God do that?"

"Well, He's truly brilliant. The more you love, the more of your heart you lose until ye get to heaven. Once there, you've not only a complete heart, but it's even bigger since all the bits of the hearts of those who love you back on earth are now part of your heavenly heart! Only in heaven can a heart hold so much love. I can't wait."

"Well, you can't die yet."

"Ha! Apparently not. God has made that one clear!"

Maeve continues to steer the stationary car in silence for a bit. After a minute, her disbelief can no longer be contained: "So, you would really only wish for one chocolate éclair?"

"No, I'd wish for two. That way I could give one to ye."

Maeve leans over and hugs Josephine before pulling back and kissing her soft old cheek.

Josephine holds the smiling round face in her crooked arthritic hands. For the first time, she sees her own young image grinning back at her.

"Yer a beautiful little angel. Now, get back to drivin' before ye crash us like Fergus!"

Maeve takes control of the road once again. The rain is coming down as hard as ever. Josephine begins rummaging through her satchel.

"All of that éclair talk made me hungry. Would ye like one of the sandwiches I packed us, Maeve?"

"Sure. I'll pull over to the side of the road so we can eat."

"Good idea."

After Maeve mimes pulling onto the shoulder, Josephine hands her half of a sandwich. They say their blessing as the rain beats down on the windshield. With the Sign of the Cross, they commence dining on buttered bread and ham.

CHAPTER 21

Shoe in the Pew

Father Adrian straightens up the altar, extinguishing a candle. The rain beating against the stained-glass windows calls him to wonder about Josephine and Maeve's expedition to the caves. He says a little prayer that they are somewhere dry and not caught out in this downpour.

As he heads out of the church to the back of the Friary, something black catches his sight in Josephine's regular pew. Father Adrian meanders over to the pew and picks up a little black shoe. He surmises it must be a shoe from one of Maeve's dolls, but a doll this size would have been noticed.

He looks closer at the shoe, fascinated with the level of craftsmanship. Father Adrian remembers his own mother talking often of how well-made leprechaun's shoes are, the good fortune they can bring to the person who possesses one, or the terrible ill fortune they can bring if neglected.

The priest cannot help but imagine the bad weather coming upon Josephine and Maeve may well be due to their leaving a lucky leprechaun shoe behind.

Oh, but that is all piseoga!

Father Adrian laughs to himself as he places the shoe in the deep pocket of his brown habit and goes on his way.

CHAPTER 22

Fall From Grace

Maeve and Josephine stare forlornly at the torrents of rain cascading down the windshield. Josephine's joints are getting stiffer by the minute. Between the dampness in the air and being cooped up in the car for such a long time, her back, neck, and legs throb with an ever-increasing level of pain. She starts to rub her knees, but ceases when her hands begin to ache.

"Auntie Jo, where is Fergus?"

"I'm not sure. He should have been back by now."

Maeve sits back in the seat with a big sigh. Josephine looks at the disappointment across the little freckled face.

"I bet ye'd like the leprechaun to give ye yer video game back now, wouldn't ye?"

Maeve's eyes light up. "Auntie Jo, give me the cell phone. We can call Mommy to pick us up and while we wait, I could play the games that are on the phone!"

Josephine begins rummaging through her purse. "Ye can play on the mobile, but we'll not bother yer mam at work. Fergus will be back here eventually."

Josephine pulls out the cell phone and hands it to Maeve, who begins pulling up one of her favorite games.

Josephine rearranges the remaining items in her purse and notices there is only one little shoe in the bag. The hair on her neck tingles as she searches more thoroughly.

"Maeve, did ye take one of the leprechaun shoes out to look at it?"

"No."

"Oh, no, we're missing one of the leprechaun shoes! No wonder the rain won't stop, we've brought ourselves a heap of bad luck now."

"Where could it be, Auntie Jo?"

"I remember! I did pull it out when the mobile rang in church. The shoe must be layin' there in our pew…right where I left it."

These words reverberate in Maeve's head. "Right where I LEFT it!"

At that moment, Maeve unlocks the riddle.

"Auntie Jo, the other right shoe is now the left shoe! We have to go back! I know the answer to the riddle! Someone else might find it and then I'll never get my wish."

Josephine checks the road for Fergus, but all she sees are rain and mud.

"Maeve, climb back there and see if there's a brelly under the seat."

"An umbrella?"

"Yes, see if one's there."

"Wouldn't Fergus have taken it if he had one?"

"Fergus isn't the quickest dog in the hunt. Go on, have a look."

Maeve searches under all the seats, but no luck.

Josephine leans over to the driver's side and pulls the lever she saw Fergus use earlier to pop the boot. That motion alone brings on a searing pain in Josephine's hands. She uses both hands to squeeze the car door handle and push the door open, but the rest of her body refuses to cooperate any further. Maeve notices Josephine's difficulty.

"I'll go look, Auntie Jo."

"Oh, thank you darlin'."

Maeve hops out and braves the drops on her way to the trunk. She returns with a large pink and orange umbrella.

"I found one!"

"Grand! Now take my hand and help me out of this jail cell."

Maeve is now an expert on how to grab Josephine's arthritic hands without squeezing her swollen joints. After three rocks to and fro, Josephine is on her feet with the final pull. She leans on Maeve, trying to straighten her crumbled frame.

"Are you okay, Auntie Jo?"

"I'll be fine. We can't be more than a mile from the Friary. A little walkin' will do me good."

Josephine takes a gander at the brightly colored brelly. "Pink and Orange? Fergus is a strange little bird, he is."

The two pilgrims make their soggy way in search of the "left" shoe. Even with the big umbrella, the rain shooting from all possible angles drenches them within minutes of their trek.

With every step that Josephine takes, pain radiates from her heels, up her legs, across her back, and out through her head and hands.

Maeve senses her discomfort and tries to prop Josephine up by folding her own arm under Josephine's. Maeve looks over at Josephine's face. The aged soft cheeks are streaked with the trail of drops. Though the rain, not tears, is the cause, Maeve sees the look of pain in Josephine's eyes.

Josephine taps into her mind over matter, calling within herself to the Blessed Mother and Jesus to give her the strength to walk to the Friary.

They make it to the point in the road where they turn east toward Clonmel.

"Less than a mile and we'll be there."

As Josephine takes her next step, her foot slips in some mud, causing her to tumble onto the turf.

Maeve stands stunned. "Auntie Jo!"

Josephine lies still and quiet. Maeve drops the umbrella and rushes to her aide. She picks Josephine's head up and holds it in her lap.

"Auntie Jo, are you okay?"

Josephine opens her eyes. "Yes, darlin'. Let me rest for a moment."

The rain is beating down hard. Maeve lays Josephine's head down and fetches the umbrella. She holds it over Josephine while she prays.

"Please God, let Auntie Jo be all right. Please let her be able to get up and make it back to town. Please, God, help us."

The rain pummels the pink and orange canopy. A screech from high above beckons Maeve's attention. She looks past the drops to a streak in the sky. The rain blurs her vision, but Maeve can see the great white owl flying overhead. "Please help us, Owl."

At that moment Maeve hears the cell phone playing out

Some Enchanted Evening. She fumbles for the purse on the other side of Josephine. Maeve reaches the ringing lifeline and answers it. "Mommy?"

It's not Micheleen.

"Fergus? Fergus! Hurry, we need help. Auntie Jo has fallen and is hurt. Yes, we just turned off that road and are going toward Clonmel."

Maeve looks back over her shoulder and sees the headlights of a car coming down the road toward them.

"Yes, I see you."

Maeve waves the car down through the pouring rain. The car stops and Fergus jumps out of the passenger side to tend to Josephine. Maeve crouches down, continuing to shield Josephine from the rain with the umbrella.

Another man gets out of the driver's side and puts his hand on Maeve's shoulder. Maeve turns to see who has touched her.

"Daddy!"

Maeve hugs her father with every ounce of her strength. "Daddy, please help Auntie Jo! She's really hurt."

James kneels next to the elderly frame. He feels the side of her neck and opens her eyelids to check for dilation. Josephine keeps her eyes open wide and looks hard at James.

"It's himself, isn't it?! Ye've some timin', James."

James smiles as he checks over the rest of the old woman's limbs. "Can you move your legs?"

Josephine does a scissor motion with her legs.

"And your arms?"

Josephine raises them over her head.

James watches her movements. "Good. Would you like to try to get up?"

Fergus and James help Josephine to her feet.

"Does anything hurt?"

"Other than my body? No."

Josephine starts trying to walk to the car. James takes her by the arm. "Auntie Jo, please forgive me."

Josephine turns and looks at James. "For what?"

"For this."

James scoops the spindly old bird up and carries her to the car. Fergus opens the back door so James can gently place Josephine in the backseat.

Josephine brushes a lock of silver hair from her flustered face. James smiles down at her coyly as he closes the car door.

Josephine remains speechless as a schoolgirl blush lingers. She cannot help but notice how handsome James is. Tall, strapping with dark hair, flashing eyes and strong, bushy black eyebrows. James would make a woman of any age melt once he set his eyes on her.

Josephine mutters to herself, "Old potato indeed."

Maeve sits in the back with Josephine but leans over the front with her arms clasped around her father's neck. Fergus sits shotgun, navigating them home.

"Daddy, you told me you were coming tomorrow!"

"I wanted to surprise you. Just by luck, I found Fergus, who brought me to you."

"I think it was more than luck." Maeve smiles.

Fergus turns to look at the backseat crowd. "Yer dah was looking for directions to Clonmel in Harrigans just as I was there getting help. We overheard each other's plights and compared stories. What a coincidence!"

Josephine corrects Fergus, "There's no such thing as a coincidence."

Maeve squeezes her father's neck tight. "I love you, Daddy."

James tries to stay on the left side of the road amongst the sheets of falling water. Fergus gives warning of the upcoming turn.

"At the next roundabout ye'll be takin' Waterford Road."

"No Fergus, we need to stop at the Friary first," interjects Josephine.

"The Friary? Haven't ye attempted enough excursions for one day, woman?"

James looks in the rearview mirror at his elder passenger. "Auntie Jo, if you don't mind, I'd like to get you back home to have a better look at the side of your face. There's some bruising and I want to make sure it's nothing serious."

"My face?" Josephine strains to see herself in the mirror but cannot.

"Don't worry, you're still young and beautiful. I want a closer look though under some decent lighting. Besides, you and Maeve are drenched. You both need to get out of those wet clothes."

Josephine sits back in her seat. "James, don't be fooled by my youthful appearance, we Irish are always older than we look. Ye are right though; we should get out of these clothes first."

Fergus rolls his eyes at Josephine's change in tone and her obvious crush on this American pretty boy. Maeve takes her arms away from her father's neck and turns to Josephine.

"But Auntie Jo?!"

"Trust me, darlin', it'll be there. We'll have yer father drive us there after we change."

Maeve sits back in a bit of a huff before looking at the side of Josephine's face. The bruise on the saggy cheek is very red and seems to be getting bigger and redder.

"Hurry up, Daddy."

Josephine pats Maeve on the hand. "He's doing fine. We don't want him drivin' like Fergus, now do we?"

Fergus throws a snide look back to Josephine. She smiles back. Diviling Fergus is always good sport.

The rain finally begins to lighten up. Fergus directs James to Waterford Road.

James pulls off to the side and lets Fergus out at the edge of town.

"Thanks so much for the lift, James. Ye just continue on about another mile..."

"Fergus! I can direct James to my own house!"

Fergus curls his nostrils at Josephine's insistence.

Josephine's voice softens. "Go on James, I'll tell ye where to turn."

James and Maeve wave good-bye to Fergus as he scurries with the undertaker's make-up and his colored brelly through the now-tamed sprinkles back to Whelan's Undertaker and Bar.

Once the crew is safe and dry in Castlecottage, James kneels next to Josephine seated on her couch and examines her bruised face. He gently touches her swollen red cheek.

"Does this hurt?"

"No."

"How about here?"

"No."

"I believe your cheek is fine."

"Are ye sure? No need to stop looking." Josephine holds up the other side of her face for him to touch.

James completes his visual exam.

"Nothing is broken, just an impressive hematoma. Let's put some ice on it to bring the swelling down.

"Maeve, get me some of the holy water from my purse and a rag. That will do the trick."

Maeve brings the small ounce-size bottle and a towel, handing them to James.

James is wary. "This water isn't even cold."

"No need fer temperature. The holiness will do the mendin.'"

James looks skeptically at Maeve who gives a nod. He pours some water on the towel and hands it to Josephine.

Josephine pushes the towel back to James.

"No, ye put the rag to my cheek. I'll just say a prayer."

Josephine blesses herself and mumbles as James awkwardly holds the damp towel to the side of her face.

Josephine looks to James. "Should be better."

James pulls the cloth away revealing a visibly less swollen, less purple bruise. He looks at the rag in disbelief.

Maeve lights up. "Yay! Okay, let's go to the Friary, Auntie Jo!"

James puts his foot down. "Maeve, holy water or not, Auntie Jo needs to lie down and rest."

"Maeve, the doctor is right. I need to rest. How could I not take his advice? He's a true oil painting, that one is. Ye show your dah the way to the Friary."

"But what if it's already gone?"

"Don't worry, dearie. You'll find it."

"Alright, Daddy, come on!"

Maeve takes her father's hand and leads him out of the cottage.

The door shuts, leaving Josephine alone, just like she had

been for the past three years since Teddy died. But for some reason, the silence right now is louder than ever. As the lack of noise rings out, the pain in her joints hums and throbs.

Josephine is no amateur at pain and solitude. She calls up the soothing image of Dr. James, bringing an immediate relief to the twisted old bones. "Old potato, indeed."

CHAPTER 23

MIXED EMOTIONS

As James and Maeve walk up to the friary doors, James debates whether to say anything about her church-going. He's not sure how he feels about her being immersed in Catholic culture, but decides not to dampen her spirits with an interrogation on his first day here.

Maeve leads James into the darkened church. Though the lights are low, the setting sun blazes through the brilliant stained-glass window behind the altar, making it all that much more glorious. James has a flashback to the days when his own grandmother, Nanny, used to take him to church.

James' parents were not devoted Catholics, only attending church themselves on Christmas, Easter, and for the occasional family wedding, baptism, or funeral. They had never pushed the Catholic faith on any of their children, but they did not mind little James going with Nanny to Mass on a weekly basis. None of the other grandchildren were willing to go with her. This made James special in her eyes, and James knew it.

Besides, he enjoyed the Mass and praying with Nanny. But when his grandmother died, so did James' connection to the Catholic Church.

As Maeve and James walk deeper into the church, a wicked face takes shape in his memory – the priest who had presided over Nanny's funeral.

James replays the memory in his mind as a lump forms in his throat.

He had gone up to his grandmother's open casket to say his goodbyes. In her hands was her rosary, the very one he had used in Mass alongside her.

James had knelt at the casket, crying, next to his mother who tried to comfort him. He turned to her and asked, "Mom, can I have Nanny's rosary?"

His mother looked at the anguish in his face and then reached in to remove the rosary from her mother's lifeless hand. Before she could hand James the sentimental string of white prayer beads, a claw of evil swiped them away.

"Don't touch these! They have been blessed and are to be buried with the departed."

"Excuse me, Father, but that is my mother's rosary. She would have wanted my son to have it."

"A rosary is not a toy. It is a holy instrument of faith. I won't allow it to be taken."

James never set foot in a Catholic Church again. Until today.

Being here now with his daughter was causing all the wonderful moments he shared with Nanny to come flooding back: the feeling of closeness to her, the feeling of being special and loving God because she loved God, the sense of pride he knew she felt whenever he went with her into this Holy place. He remembers how over and over again she would tell him she couldn't wait till the day she could watch him make his First Holy Communion.

She never saw him make it. And he never did.

James feels a tug on his right hand. He looks down at Maeve's excited little face.

"Isn't this place beautiful, Daddy? God is here."

"Yes, Sweetie, it is."

Maeve pulls James along to the right of the sacristy where she and Josephine sit. As they come upon the pew, Maeve's heart sinks. The seat is empty. The shoe is gone.

"Oh no."

"It's not there? Are you sure this is the pew?"

"Yes, I'm sure. We need to find Father Adrian. He might know…"

"Where ye left yer shoe?" Father Adrian's voice chimes in as he approaches from behind them.

Maeve lunges for the friar. "Do you have it, Father Adrian?"

"Well, that depends. I found a shoe, but I must make sure tis yers 'fore I hand it over. Can ye describe the one yer missin'?"

Maeve plays along with as much patience as she can muster.

"It's a small, black, right shoe with a gold buckle."

Father Adrian pulls the little shoe out from his large brown pocket. "Wait a minute, did ye say a right shoe? I'm afraid that's not correct. This must not be yers."

He starts to put the shoe back in his pocket.

"What? Let me see it."

Father Adrian holds out the tiny article of footwear.

"Ye see, I have a left shoe and yer lookin' for a right one. This one must belong to someone else."

Maeve feigns ignorance. "Sorry, I meant left shoe. I get my rights and lefts mixed up sometimes."

Father Adrian smiles as he hands the perfect little shoe over to Maeve. Maeve is convinced more than ever that her wish will be granted now that the two shoes make a real honest to goodness pair.

Father Adrian extends his hand to James, "Father Adrian. Are ye Maeve's father?"

"Yes, James Costello. Nice to meet you, Father."

Father Adrian addresses Maeve. "Did ye and yer Auntie make it to the caves or did the showers wash ye out?"

"We didn't go. Auntie Jo had a bad fall, but Daddy and Fergus found us and got her out."

"A fall?! Is Josephine all right?"

"Daddy's a doctor. He took care of her."

James fills the priest in. "She's a bit banged up, but nothing is broken. I've told her to get some rest and she'll be fine."

"Ye told her to rest? She bein' a faith healer, I can't imagine she takes to a medical doctor all that kindly."

"Auntie Jo listens to Daddy. She thinks he's an oil painting."

"An oil painting, now?" Father Adrian nudges James. "The old sayin' rings true again."

"What's that?"

"To command their duty, it helps to have beauty!"

James chuckles at the remark and marvels at how different this priest is from the one at Nanny's funeral.

Father Adrian scratches at his chin. "Oh well, this drab face must go prepare fer Vespers. Glad ye found yer leprechaun's shoe, Maeve. I know ye'll make a wise wish with it." Father Adrian gives Maeve a wink before disappearing in the shadows of the Friary.

"Why did he call it a leprechaun's shoe?"

"That's what they call these little shoes here in Ireland, leprechaun shoes."

"You've learned a lot for only being here a couple days."

"Uh-huh. Now let's get back to Auntie Jo. She doesn't like being alone."

James bends down to Maeve's level. "You know, Maeve, going to church with Auntie Jo and pretend games with leprechaun shoes can be fun, but remember this is make-believe stuff. Never let yourself be fooled into thinking this is real."

"Daddy, don't worry, I love you. That's what is real."

James rises, looking down at his daughter's toothy grin. "I love you too, Maeve."

CHAPTER 24

Peas in a Pod

Micheleen walks into the cottage to find Josephine curled up on the sofa, asleep, with an open-mouthed, gap-toothed grin spread across her face. Out of the corner of her mouth is a thin trickle of drool dribbling down the side of her chin, pooling in a small ring on the well-worn flowered couch.

"Auntie Jo? Auntie Jo."

Josephine slowly emerges from slumber, "Yes, dearie? I'm sorry, I didn't even know I'd nodded off." Josephine focuses on Micheleen who looks like herself for the first time: no false eyelashes, no makeup. "You look pretty without those millipedes dancing on yer face."

Micheleen pulls back, "Millipedes?"

Josephine motions, fluttering her fingers over her eyes.

"Oh, I didn't have time to put my lashes on this morning."

"You shouldn't ever bother."

"ANYWAY, so he's already gone off somewhere with Maeve? Maeve texted me that he's here."

"Oh, James? Yes. They went to fetch one of the shoes we left in Mass this morning."

"A shoe? "

"One of the leprechaun shoes. I took it out to find something in my purse and forgot to put it back in."

Micheleen begins laughing out loud.

"What's so funny?"

"The thought of James having to go inside a church for starters, and for none other than to retrieve a leprechaun shoe! I can hardly wait to hear the issues he'll have over this one. Oh boy."

"I fancy he'll have no objection at all."

"You don't know him, Auntie Jo."

"Dearie, yer my blood, and I do love ye with all my heart, but now that I've seen what ye call an 'old potato,' *yer* the one I'm not sure about."

"Oh, brother." Micheleen rolls her eyes and scoffs.

"Micheleen, I'm not privy to all of the details between ye and James, but I'm old enough to peg a match. I'd hate fer ye to lose the love of yer life."

"What!?!"

Suddenly, Immaculata McClure pokes her head in the cottage door. "Hello? Josephine?"

"Mackie, come in. What are ye doin' down this way?"

"Checkin' on ye. Fergus told me ye'd had a spill on the road. I wanted to make sure ye weren't in need of anythin'."

Micheleen whips her head in Auntie Jo's direction. "What spill on the road?"

"I also wanted to get a load of Dr. Handsome. Fergus told us ye were makin' eyes at him."

Josephine ignores Micheleen's question, instead focusing on denying her crush to Immaculata. "Fergus is daft. I was makin' eyes at no one."

Immaculata nudges Micheleen. "I'd watch her, ye know, she tried to steal my man once."

"Immaculata!"

Immaculata covers her mouth, pretending to hold back her glee as Josephine swats the air in Immaculata's direction. She finds it too painful to reach far enough to land a blow. Micheleen stands perplexed.

"Fergus said he's a regular Cary Grant. The girls down at the bank are plannin' on showin' up at the pub tonight in hopes of meetin' him. Ye'll have to bring him in, Josephine."

"Oh, not tonight, Mack. I really am quite banged up from my fall."

Micheleen pleads for the update. "What fall? Somebody tell me what happened!"

"'Tis nothing. I slipped a little in the mud on the side of the road."

Micheleen looks closer at Josephine's face. "Your face is a little bruised."

"James already looked at it. I'm fine. I just need to rest this evenin'."

Josephine turns to Immaculata. "Tell the girls I'll bring him in tomorrow for them to gander. But just to look, not to touch. They're to keep their distance. He's not up fer auction quite yet."

"Why? Whom are ye holding him for?" Immaculata glances in Micheleen's direction.

"Not for me! He's fair game," Micheleen protests, throwing her hands up.

"Fair? He's gorgeous! It's little Maeve I'm thinkin' of. I don't think she'd take kindly to a gaggle of beautiful young girls swarmin' over her dah."

"Why does James garner a bevy of beauties? Where are the throngs of eligible bachelors coming out to meet me?" Micheleen questions.

Immaculata and Josephine share a glance. Immaculata fills in the blanks. "Darlin', don'tch ye know? Yer an American woman in Ireland. The men here have to know ye at the minimum of a decade before one will dare ask ye out, and that's only after his mother and every livin' female relative okay's ye first. Ye'll be an old grey mare before yer fitted for a saddle here."

Micheleen's mouth drops open. "Uh-excuse me?"

"It's the truth, Micheleen. Irish men aren't Romeos, unless of course yer shootin' for one in his 70's. I could have ye married in the week if that's the age husband ye want."

"I'm afraid to ask...what changes when they hit 70?"

"That's about the time their mothers have finally passed away. Before that happens, you've a series of hoops to jump, and being an American only doubles the course."

"My father didn't wait for decades to marry my mother."

"That's because there was the Atlantic Ocean between him and his mother. If it's an Irish husband ye want, yer best bet is to go to America to get him," Immaculata says.

Josephine pipes in: "No, her best bet is to get a second helpin' of boiled potatoes."

Micheleen crosses her arms as she scoffs, "Gross. I'd rather starve."

The door opens. James pokes his head in. "Who's hungry?"

Maeve darts through the door past James as he continues in with an enormous bag of take-out food.

"Maeve and I passed the Chinese restaurant on our way back, so I figured I'd pick up some dinner. Hello Meesh."

"James."

James holds the bag up. "I think there's enough here to feed all of us."

Immaculata whispers to Josephine. "Especially since Micheleen won't be eating any. Jo, yer right, he is gorgeous."

Micheleen rolls her eyes as the two hens cackle over the new rooster in the yard. She takes the bag from James and begins sorting out the selection of containers on the kitchen table. James helps her get the dishes and utensils out.

Maeve runs to Josephine's purse and fishes out the right leprechaun shoe, presenting the shoes for Josephine to see side by side.

"Sure, ye have ye a right and a left! Oh Maeve, true enchantment!"

"So, what do I do now?"

Josephine pulls Maeve off to the side of the couch and whispers. "Ye must leave these out at the back door overnight. Ye write the answer to the riddle on a slip of paper and put it in the left shoe. Then write yer wish on another slip of paper and put it in the right shoe. The shoes will be gone in the mornin'. Expect yer wish to be granted before noon."

"What if he doesn't take the shoes?"

"Do what I told ye and he'll take them, not to worry."

Maeve's eyes beam with delight for a flash, but grow dim almost immediately. "Will you help me?"

"After our meal we'll sneak away from yer parents and write

the notes. Now, go help them get the food ready. I smell the Kung Pao chicken. Hurry, I'm hurt, and I'm famished!"

Maeve goes to help set the table while Immaculata sits down next to Josephine on the couch to better observe the unwilling couple.

"They're suited to a 'T', Jo."

"I know it, Mack. The moment I saw him I was sure they were matched."

"Yer niece needs to see the sharks swarmin' around Dr. Good-looking. She'll wise up quick."

Josephine agrees, "She needs to see his soul. She's wearin' blinders and somethin' needs to take them off. One riddle down, one more to go."

"What riddle down?"

"Oh, nothing."

Immaculata looks back at Micheleen and James, "Look at the two of 'em. Peas in a pod."

Josephine's stomach growls.

"Micheleen, is my Chinese ready? Ye can fix me a plate with a bit of everythin', but I fancy the Kung Pao Chicken so don't be stingy. James, come help me up. I'm feeling the ramifications of my tumble."

James makes a suggestion, "I can bring a plate to you, so you don't have to get up."

"No eating outside the kitchen in my house! Were ye brought up in a barn, James?"

"No, ma'am. I wasn't thinking."

Micheleen fixes Josephine a plate as James does the honors of escorting the walking wounded to the table. As all take a seat, Maeve makes the Sign of the Cross and leads the blessing. "Bless us oh Lord…"

James' eyes widen. He's surprised that his daughter already has a prayer memorized. The shock is quickly washed away by a wave of sadness, as he realizes the words coming from his daughter's mouth are the same he used to repeat before meals at Nanny's house.

James joins in at the end by making the Sign of the Cross.

Josephine looks to Micheleen with raised eyebrows. Micheleen shrugs her shoulders and then eyes James.

James looks at the circle of faces staring at him. "When in Rome..."

Micheleen smiles.

Maeve revels in this moment while Immaculata and Josephine lock eyes with each other, diving into a ready-made conversation over the need for a decent Italian restaurant in town.

As the meal ends, Immaculata helps Micheleen clean up. James aids Josephine in her efforts to make it back to the couch. Maeve grabs Josephine's other arm to help her, too.

Micheleen takes this moment to lay down the rules. "Maeve, your father and I are meeting with the headmaster of a school tomorrow. I want you and Auntie Jo to stay here until we get back. No going anywhere, not Mass, not Patrick's Well, not the Holy Spot, not even down by the river. Do you understand?

Josephine jumps in, "Micheleen, not to worry. This old body is stayin' put for the next couple days. That tumble has taken its toll on me."

Maeve cannot hide her disappointment. "A couple days? You'll feel better by tomorrow, Auntie Jo, I can tell. Your bruise looks smaller already. Why don't you let me sprinkle more of the Patrick's Well water on you? That will make your pain go away."

"Oh darlin', I wish that was all it took. Unfortunately, that spill was more than this old body is used to."

Josephine sneezes.

A chorus rings out, "Bless you."

Josephine dabs her nose with a napkin. "I'm a healer, but only of others. I can't mend as quickly as I once did." She sneezes again.

Dread strikes Maeve as she remembers her mean-spirited proclamation from that first day when Auntie Jo was the target of her hatred: *I wish she would catch a cold... and die. Maybe then we could go home.* She fears her earlier wish may have been applied on her now beloved friend.

Maeve relives her mother's look of horror that day on the river path.

"Maeve..." Micheleen's voice in the living room brings Maeve back to the present. "You have your new computer to play on tomorrow. You haven't even checked out the games I had loaded on it."

"That's no fun anymore."

Josephine sniffles as she grabs Maeve's hand.

"Maeve, I'll be better by the weekend. We'll go to Mass together and then ye can show yer parents some of our spots."

"Even the Holy Spot?"

Josephine inhales deeply, knowing another miracle would be needed for her to get up there again.

"Give me a day or two."

Maeve gently hugs her stiff wrinkly neck. She pulls back and looks at her favorite new, but elderly, friend. "Okay."

Immaculata puts a final glass back in the cupboard. "I'll be off to the pub now. Thank ye, James, for the Chinese. Shall I tell the folks ye will all make an appearance tomorrow eve?"

Josephine strains to look back over her shoulder at Immaculata. "I make no promises. Check in with me in the afternoon, I'll know how my old bones are feelin' by then."

Immaculata throws her hand in the air in farewell. "Take care all, I'll check with ye, Jo." She shuts the door as the final fingers of sunlight wave good-bye to a long Irish spring day.

With the dimming of daylight, James senses it's almost time for him to leave. He is not ready to say goodnight. He had seen Micheleen smile, and he longs to make that happen again.

"So where is the white owl your father used to talk about? Didn't he say it lived in the castle ruin?"

Micheleen looks over to Maeve. "You should ask your daughter about the owl. She nearly flew away with it the first day we were here."

"Maeve, will you go out with us to look for it?"

Maeve shakes her head back and forth.

Josephine wraps her arms around Maeve's shoulders. "The owl gave Maeve quite a scare her first day. For over a hundred years now the bird has been touted as a great protector of Castlecottage, though to me it's always seemed a bit of a show-off. The bloody thing will wake me up at the crack of dawn just to warn me of some omen, good or bad—as if an old woman needs an owl to signal such things! The aches in my bones tell me just as much. If ye wish to see it, go out and stand at the gate frontin' the trees. Watch the top of the castle keep. The owl should be perchin' up there in the next ten minutes, surveyin' before goin' off for its nightly hunt."

James begs Maeve to accompany them one more time. "Are you sure you won't come out with us?"

"I've seen it already. Mommy can show you."

James looks at Micheleen, eyebrows raised.

"Oh, all right," the reluctant Micheleen groans.

James holds the door as Micheleen leads the way to the front yard and castle gate. She walks him over to the primary viewing location.

"You should see him any minute over there." Micheleen points to the top of the castle keep.

James leans against the gate and looks over at her.

"Are you happy, Meesh?"

Micheleen looks back at him. "What do you mean?"

"You brought our daughter all the way over to Ireland to take a promotion... a promotion that you couldn't have cared less about a year ago. It seems like you're running from something...or someone. So...now that you're here...Are you happy?"

Micheleen's face turns bright red.

"I am NOT running from anything...or anyone." She glares in James' direction. "After everything I've been through the past year, I needed a fresh start...*we* needed a fresh start."

A tear starts to form in the corner of her eye. "Maeve and I are adjusting well, and yes, we're happy."

James shuffles his feet in the grass. "I'm glad to hear that, Meesh. You deserve to be happy."

He takes a step closer to Micheleen and gently grabs her arm.

"You're the most intelligent woman I know. You will do amazing things for your company here in Ireland."

Micheleen looks James in the eyes. He reaches out and touches her face with the back of his index finger. "And you're still as beautiful as the day we met."

Micheleen's body tenses and her lips flatten. She pushes him away. "You just don't get it at all, James! Ugh!"

She storms away towards the cottage, pounding her feet on the cobblestone pathway.

CHAPTER 25

The Wish is in The Writing

A loud slam of the front door shakes the house. Maeve and Josephine's eyes dart to the other end of the room to see a red-faced Micheleen standing in the hall by the thoroughly closed front door. A car can be heard spewing gravel as it screeches out of the front courtyard and up the tree-lined drive.

Josephine winces and whispers to Maeve. "Looks like yer wish took two steps back."

Maeve runs to Micheleen. "What's wrong, Mommy?"

Micheleen smooths her shirt and brushes her hair out of her face.

"Nothing. Daddy says good night. He'll come see you tomorrow afternoon after our meeting with the headmaster. You should get to bed now, honey. Go get in your pajamas and I'll be in there in a minute."

Maeve presses her hands together in a prayer position while begging, "Mommy, can I please finish writing out the answer to the leprechaun riddle with Auntie Jo?"

Micheleen exhales slowly. "Honey, I'm really tired. It's been a long day…"

"Micheleen, ye can go. I'll ensure the wee one goes to bed as soon as we're done."

"Alright. Thanks, Auntie Jo."

Micheleen gives Maeve a hug and kiss goodnight. "Auntie Jo needs to rest. You finish up quickly and get straight to bed on your own."

"Okay, Mommy. Goodnight."

Josephine and Maeve wait until Micheleen is out of earshot.

"Okay, Maeve, now that you've got the pair of shoes and solved the riddle, get a piece of paper and a pen. The wish is in the writin'."

Maeve fetches the supplies to complete the mission, handing them to Auntie Jo.

"First, we must ask God to bless this wish." Josephine makes the Sign of the Cross. "Lord, please look kindly on this simple wish. May it only be in line with Your Holy Will. Please keep all dark forces from taking part and keep our hearts and wishes in Your hands at all times. Amen."

Maeve repeats, "Amen."

"Now, it must be written in yer hand. I'll help ye with any words ye don't know how to spell. Then ye place the notes in the shoes and set them outside."

Maeve thinks out loud, "We had to leave the right shoe to make it a left shoe. How would I say that?"

"Hmmm, how about this…To make a proper pair from two right shoes, one right shoe must be left?"

"That sounds good, Auntie Jo."

Auntie Jo helps Maeve write out the answer to the riddle.

"Ok, now what do ye want to write for yer wish?"

Maeve hesitates.

"What's the matter, darlin'?"

"I thought if you tell someone your wish it might not come true."

"Hmm, that's a good point. Why don't ye write it out as best as ye can. I'm sure it will be good enough."

Maeve carefully writes out her wish on the second piece of paper and then places both notes in the shoes.

"Now set the shoes outside the back door. He'll come get them just after the stroke of midnight."

"How do you know?"

"'Tis the witchin' hour. That is the only time when ghost, fairy, elf, and all things enchanted and mystical can move about without the fear of being captured by a human. People can see them then, but durin' the first few minutes of every day they remain untouchable to us."

"How do they know when the witching hour is over?"

"When a match can be lit, they know they've overstayed their welcome. Ye can light a candle before the witching hour and it will stay lit, but during the witching hour, no new light can be made. Ye can strike and strike and ye'd swear yer matches were wet as a fish. Not a spark ye'll get till the witching hour passes. Mind ye, it's only for a few minutes, five at the most, dependin' on the season."

Maeve opens the back door and puts the two little shoes on the stoop.

"Okay, dearie, it's time for ye to get to bed."

Maeve yawns. "Do you need me to help you get to bed, Auntie Jo?"

"That's sweet of ye to offer, but I'm going to sleep on the couch tonight. My bones are telling me to stay put here."

"Can I get you anything else?"

Josephine pauses to think. "Would ye mind bringin' me my pillow and a blanket?"

Maeve retrieves the items and makes sure Josephine is comfortable before heading off to bed. On her way, she quietly grabs Josephine's cell phone from her purse and shields it in the palm of her hand.

Once Maeve's door closes and the light from under her door goes dark, Josephine looks up to her crucifix and ends her evening in prayer.

Though her body throbs with dull pain throughout every joint, she can tell the old bones are more tired than injured.

It doesn't take long for Josephine to sink into a slumber, rescuing her from the discomfort of waking agedness.

Maeve lies in her bed staring at the glow being thrown off of her untouched computer. Saint Mary stands next to it, the light shining from the computer onto the little statue. Maeve smiles back at her before pulling Auntie Jo's cell phone out from under her sheets. She sets an alarm for 11:55 p.m. before laying her head down on her pillow and closing her eyes.

CHAPTER 26

NOT SO SAGE, SAGE ADVICE

The baby-faced barman pours a glass of Jameson's whiskey and slides it in front of his lone customer. James throws it back then looks to the barman for another.

"How much longer until you close?"

"Sir, as a guest of the Hotel Minella, yer welcome to sit in here all night. I'm on duty for as long as ye are here."

James stares at the half empty bottle of whiskey in front of him. "Just pour me one more. That will do."

"Yes sir."

The barman studies James as he pours the honey-colored liquid into a shot glass.

"I'm assuming yer here over a woman."

James sighs and then hiccups. "Is it that obvious?"

"As obvious as an elephant in yer living room. If ye don't

mind me askin', did ye try telling her how gorgeous she is? That seems to werk fer most lads."

James looks at the barman and laughs.

"If you can believe it, that's exactly what got her mad at me! I happen to be in love with the one woman on the planet who apparently doesn't want to hear she's smart and beautiful."

The barman slaps his towel on the bar.

"Well then, that's yer whole problem! She wants none of the pressure of being perfect for ye. Don't go showin' yer hand, man! Keep her guessin'. A little fabricated jealousy never hurts neither. Sometimes lasses don't realize what they have until it's almost gone."

James looks back up at the young man. The barman returns his gaze with one red eyebrow raised.

"It may be the whiskey talking, but I think you may be on to something, Red."

James slams his glass on the bar after polishing off his final swallow.

CHAPTER 27

Tell No Smell

A soft fluttering noise rustles by the bedroom window. Maeve rolls over, recognizing the sound of the white owl's wings. Rubbing her eyes, she gets up and goes to the window. The owl hoots to her from the stonewall, swiveling its head toward the backdoor.

Maeve rushes over to check the cell phone clock. It reads 11:58. The alarm never sounded! *I must have set it for a.m. instead of p.m.!*

Through the darkness, Maeve quickly makes her way down the hall and across the pitch-black kitchen. She cautiously feels for the kitchen door, being careful not to wake Auntie Jo on the couch.

When she opens the door, she breathes a sigh of relief at the sight of the little shoes still lying on the mat. Something rustles in the bushes beyond the garden. Maeve grabs the shoes along with the notes, locks the deadbolt, and scurries back to her room.

Josephine wakes at 12:30 a.m. She goes to open the stoop door and finds that the shoes are gone. She assumes a leprechaun must have taken a liking to them and heads back to the couch.

CHAPTER 28

A WISH GRANTED

Josephine awakens. She expects to be sore from sleeping on the couch all night, but she sits up with ease, without any pain. Upon standing, she's greeted with a strange burst of energy.

At that moment, Maeve emerges from her bedroom and hesitantly walks in to the living room. "Auntie Jo? How do you feel this morning?"

"It's the strangest thing. I feel great! I'm not sure how it's possible, but I feel even better than I did a couple days ago! I sure hope this doesn't mean Father. Adrian feels worse." Josephine's forehead wrinkles deepen as worry sets in.

"Wow! It worked! It really worked!"

"What worked? What do ye mean?"

"This is exactly what I asked for!" Maeve starts jumping up and down. "I decided not to ask the leprechaun to get my parents back together."

"But Maeve! What about yer mam and dah?"

"I decided to leave them to God." Maeve smiles. "Now you're well enough to play again today."

Josephine turns to Maeve and hugs her tight, "Oh Maeve, thank you!"

"So, what do you want to do first, Auntie Jo? Go up to the Holy Spot and look for fairies?"

"Yes! But let's go change first. I'll race ye upstairs." Josephine exclaims.

The two race up the stairs and head for Josephine's room. Josephine moves more like an 18-year-old than an 80-year-old. When she gets to the room, she climbs onto the big, springy bed and begins bouncing. "I haven't done this since I was a wee one!"

Maeve joins her and the two bounce as high as they can. Suddenly, a loud bang erupts as the slats of the old bed give way and the bottom end buckles with a thud.

Maeve's eyes get big as saucers. "Uh-oh, we're in trouble now."

Josephine looks at her. "With whom are we in trouble? Auntie Jo?"

The two giggle with delight, wallowing in the knowledge that the patients run the asylum on this miraculous day.

After they change clothes, Josephine grabs Maeve's hand. "Off to the covered wood. The fairies are waitin'!"

Maeve swats at Josephine: "Tag! You're it!" The pair gallop down the twisty wooden stairs, laughing and yelling like banshees the whole way down the hall. With every step, Josephine feels the amazing agility of a youthful body.

The pair bolts out the door and up the lane, heading toward the cross on the hill and the little covered wood.

"Slow down, Maeve. Even though I feel better than I have in decades, I still can't quite keep up with ye!"

Maeve slows down to catch her breath and smiles at the sight of the young-feeling Auntie Jo. On the outside she looks the same, but she is standing taller and the twinkle in her eyes is brighter.

Josephine and Maeve spend the morning exploring the fairy wood. Today, Josephine feels agile enough to crouch through the tunnel and zoom down the slide.

"C'mon, Auntie Jo! Let's go explore over here!" Maeve pulls Josephine across the field and then plops down on the grass. "This is the best day ever!"

"I agree!" Josephine plops down next to Maeve and marvels at how easy it is for her to move about.

"Hey, are ye getting hungry? We could go get some lunch at O'Connor's. I have a hankerin' fer some more of that shepherd's pie."

"I'm starving! Let's go!" Maeve pulls Josephine's arm to help her stand, even though the assistance is not needed today.

They make their way down to town and giggle like two little schoolgirls walking into the restaurant. The hostess seats them at a table in the corner.

The waiter that Josephine spewed water all over a few days ago walks up to the table hesitantly.

"Hello ladies, I'm Simon, and I'll be yer server this afternoon. What can I get ye to drink?"

Maeve chimes in immediately. "I'll take an Irish lemonade, please."

"Well, I'm glad ye like the Irish kind, because that's the only kind we carry. And for ye, mam?" Simon turns to Josephine.

"I'll take an Irish lemonade too." She winks at Maeve.

A few minutes later, Simon delivers the drinks and takes their food order.

Maeve slurps a giant swig of lemonade through her straw. Josephine sees her younger self across the table and smirks. Maeve returns the gesture with a huge gap-toothed smile.

"Maeve," Josephine begins slowly. "There is something I've got to tell ye." She swallows hard, past the rising lump in her throat.

"It means so much to me that ye chose to use yer leprechaun wish on me instead of yer parents. I haven't had someone do somethin' so nice for me in a very long time."

A tear begins to form in the corner of her eye.

"You're welcome, Auntie Jo." Maeve smiles again. "But there's something that I've got to tell you too." She takes another swig of the lemonade, building the suspense. "I didn't make a leprechaun wish."

Josephine scrunches her face in a confused stupor. "What do ye mean?... When I woke up without pain this mornin', ye said that was what ye had asked for."

Maeve points to the entryway of the restaurant. "I asked *her*."

Josephine cranes her neck to see who Maeve could possibly be pointing to. Behind the hostess station, she sees the statue of the Blessed Mother surrounded by candles. She begins to weep. "Ye asked St. Mary to heal me?"

Maeve takes another slurp of her lemonade. "Well, I wanted you to feel better. I thought about asking the leprechaun, but I decided that asking the Blessed Mother would be better, you know, since she's so close to Jesus and all."

Josephine grabs Maeve's hand across the table. "Thank ye, dearie. Ye just gave me the most precious gift."

Josephine silently thanks the Blessed Mother for her intercession and for bringing Maeve into her life, then she makes the Sign of the Cross.

CHAPTER 29

SMALL WORLD

A bare-faced Micheleen hustles up to the reception desk of Stonebridge Academy. Her conference call ran over at work and she is now fifteen minutes late to their 11 o'clock meeting.

The woman sitting behind the mahogany counter is in no hurry to receive, pushing an array of papers from one side to the other.

"Excuse me. I have an appointment with Headmaster O'Hearne. My name is Micheleen Costello—I mean Kelly. My husband's last name is Costello, my ex-husband. Is he here?"

The receptionist exhales loudly and stares up at Micheleen with an annoyed look on her face. "Yer EX-husband is here. He's meeting with Headmistress O'Hearne already."

"Oh, good, where do I go?"

The receptionist sighs and then points down the hall. "The Headmistress' office is the last room on the left."

"Thank you."

Micheleen straightens her coiffed hair and strides past the unfriendly woman, down the long, dimly lit hall of the esteemed academic institution.

Micheleen approaches a beveled glass door with the name HEADMISTRESS MOIRA O'HEARNE emblazoned in gold letters. She can hear a woman's flirtatious laughter coming from the other side.

Micheleen opens the door and finds James and a young woman with perfectly curled auburn hair smiling at each other. O'Hearne looks up, the smile fading from her flawless porcelain face.

"Excuse me, Headmistress O'Hearne? I'm Micheleen Kelly." Micheleen stretches out her right hand.

"Sorry?"

James intervenes. "Moira, this is Maeve's mother."

"Oh, Ms. Kelly, very nice to meet ye. Please, pull up that chair over there and I'll go over what I've already told Maeve's father."

Micheleen pulls a hard wooden chair from the corner and scoots it next to James, who is seated in an oversized padded wingback.

The separate terms 'Maeve's mother' and 'Maeve's father' pinch Micheleen's ears. It's as if Maeve was an abstract science project conceived in a test tube, and Micheleen and James have no other point of reference to one another, no personal connection to one another or the family they began.

Micheleen looks at James, who is staring intently at the talking headmistress. *Has James noticed how pretty Headmistress O'Hearne is?*

Micheleen stares at the side of James' face, watching him nod intently at the Irish woman's words.

James turns to Micheleen, reprimanding her with his eyes for being late. She turns back to the headmistress, Moira O'Hearne. She's the woman James described just last night: beautiful and smart. Add to that, O'Hearne's melodic Irish accent – *who wouldn't want to listen to her talk all day?*

Micheleen glances at James, who is still taking in Moira O'Hearne's every word. *Hasn't Moira already said all of this to him before?*

Micheleen looks back at the headmistress, then down at her left hand - no ring. *Did James notice this too?...Of course he did. Have they already made a date?*

"Ms. Kelly, again, what were your expectations as far as Maeve's daily extracurricular activities now that I've told you all that we offer?"

Micheleen had heard her lovely voice, but had not listened to a single thing the woman had said.

"I'm sorry, could you list them one more time?"

Headmistress O'Hearne straightens in her padded chair. "Really?"

James jumps in. "No, she's just being funny. What we want is for Maeve to play a team sport, continue piano, maybe try the dance thing next year, right Micheleen?"

He just called me 'Micheleen.'

For as long as he has known her, even in their most heated arguments, James never called her anything but 'Meesh'.

"Micheleen?" There it was again. That word sounded so foreign on his tongue.

Micheleen responds, "Right, yes, that sounds right." *Nothing sounds right.*

Headmistress O'Hearne checks off the list on her paper and looks Micheleen up and down.

"Ye do realize we will need to have Maeve tested within the next week for admittance to be offered for next term? I know yer probably meetin' with other schools. I don't enjoy puttin' pressure on parents to decide so quickly, but we really have no choice. Here it is May, most of our classes were filled back in February."

The Headmistress gives her full attention to James. "If Maeve tests well, we can make room for her, but we need to know immediately."

Before James can respond, Micheleen pipes in.

"We want to go ahead and have her tested here at Stonebridge. I've researched all of the schools and this is our first choice. Can we go ahead and schedule the testing now?"

The Headmistress cocks her head at the now attentive woman. "Of course, can ye have Maeve here Monday morning by 8?"

"Maeve's father will have left the country by then, but I'll have her here. How long is the testing?"

James turns to Micheleen, eyebrows raised.

The Headmistress straightens up and sits a little higher in her chair. "The entire process takes roughly 5 hours."

Micheleen leans toward the Headmistress. "I'm sorry. Did you say it takes 5 *hours* to test for second grade?"

"We call it second year, and yes, 5 hours. She will have a 30-minute break, at which point we will feed her. Of course, if ye'd like to wait until you've spoken to the other schools… that is your decision."

"No, set her up for Monday."

The headmistress looks at James. He shrugs, but nods.

The Headmistress makes a note of the date on their paperwork.

"All right, ye, Ms. Kelly—not Dr. Costello—will have Maeve here promptly at 7:45 next Monday to begin testin' at 8, correct?"

"Correct, Mrs. O'Hearn."

"That's *Miss* O'Hearn. Very well then. Are there any more questions?"

Micheleen stands up. "No, I believe we're set."

The headmistress stands, as does James. She reaches out to shake James' hand and smiles coyly.

"A pleasure to meet ye, James. Small world, small, small world."

She then reaches for Micheleen's hand, "And very nice to meet ye too, Ms. Kelly."

Micheleen firmly grips the smaller Irish hand. "Thank you for meeting with us. I'll see you Monday."

The headmistress escorts them to the door and opens it. "Actually, my assistant will be taking care of the testin' Monday. I'll already be on holiday."

Micheleen feigns interest. "Really? Where are you going?"

"Coincidentally, the same place as James. Have a good day now."

The headmistress turns abruptly and closes the door before Micheleen can say another word.

Micheleen turns to James with a hard look and says quietly, "You're telling me that the hot, single headmistress 'just happens' to be vacationing in the same city as your conference next week?"

James shrugs nonchalantly, "Like she said, small world."

CHAPTER 30

Repairing the Road

James hops in his rental car and heads to Auntie Jo's cottage. As he drives, he wonders if Meesh's strange behavior at the meeting with the headmistress was from a twinge of jealousy.

He's looking forward to spending the afternoon with Maeve, but his mind is preoccupied with how to get to Meesh. He knows he screwed up and has to find a way to fix it.

James pulls in the driveway just as Auntie Jo and Maeve are walking up the path to the house. He marvels at how well Auntie Jo is walking, considering all she went through yesterday. The bruise on her face is nowhere to be found.

She's a tough one....Micheleen must get it honestly.

James parks and opens his car door.

Maeve comes running over and gives him a huge hug. "Daddy!!! Auntie Jo and I had the best morning!"

"I'm so glad to hear that." James looks to Auntie Jo. "Feeling better, are ya? You look great!"

Josephine blushes. "Thank ye, Doctor. I feel great. Thanks be to God and His little angel right there." She points to Maeve.

"Well, I'll let ye two have yer afternoon together. I think I'm going to head up to the friary to take advantage of some pain-free kneelin' and to offer up my thanks."

"Hop in the car, Auntie Jo, I'll drop you off on our way to the stadium."

"What stadium?" Maeve asks.

"Clonmel has a greyhound stadium. I thought it would be fun to take you to see a dog race this afternoon. What do you think?"

"That sounds awesome, Daddy!"

"Perfect. Let's all get in the car then."

A few minutes of a rural car drive later, James pulls up to the friary doors.

"Daddy, is it okay if I go in for a couple minutes, too? I have to go thank God for something."

James hesitates. "Uhm, I suppose that would be alright. I'll wait right here for you."

Maeve runs ahead into the church as Josephine begins to exit the car.

Realizing they are now alone, Josephine stops abruptly and turns towards James.

"James, this is not my business, but I know ye are still in love with Micheleen. Would ye mind if I gave ye a bit of advice?"

James exhales loudly. "Sure. I could use all the help I can get."

Josephine rubs her knee with her knobby hand.

"Sometimes it helps to know the moment things took a turn down the road of heartlessness. Do ye know when that was for the two of ye?"

James bites his lips and looks up, thinking. "I know she shut down after her father passed away."

"Indeed 'twas. Now the question is, why? Put yerself in her shoes at the foot of his bedside."

With that, Josephine exits the car.

"Thanks fer the ride, dearie. Be back at the house fer dinner. I'm makin' ye a roast."

CHAPTER 31

A New Taste for Hot Potato

Micheleen walks in the house while Josephine is preparing dinner.

"Hi, Auntie Jo."

She glances around and doesn't see Maeve or James. "I suppose Maeve is still out with James?"

"Yes, he took her to the greyhound races. They should be back soon."

Micheleen sets her work bag down and plops herself in one of the chairs at the kitchen table with a heavy sigh.

"Rough day, eh?"

Josephine cuts a slab of butter and places it in with the mashed potatoes.

"Ugh. Work was....well, work. But the worst part was the meeting with that headmistress today. She was so... ugh. And James was so...ugh, I don't even know. And they want to test

Maeve for five hours on Monday...for second grade! I mean, second *year*." Micheleen rolls her eyes and slams her forehead into her hands.

"Sounds to me like ye don't like seein' yer man talkin' to another woman."

Josephine stops stirring the potatoes to add a little salt and pepper.

"He's NOT my man."

"Well, regardless, ye should pay attention to yer heart. Maybe ye should think on it."

Josephine takes a taste of the spuds to see if they need anything more.

"I don't know. I'm over all the thinking." Micheleen lifts her head towards the stove. "What are you making for dinner? It smells fantastic."

"Oh, just some roast, asparagus, and...boiled potatoes."

Micheleen groans. "You've got to be kidding me."

"These boiled potatoes have been mashed, buttered, and spiced. They are going to be yer new favorite."

Josephine looks out the window above the sink and sees James' rental car approaching.

"Speakin' of potatoes..."

Micheleen sits at the dinner table listening to Maeve talk nonstop about her afternoon with her dad. Micheleen had scarfed down the succulent meat and crispy asparagus, leaving only the mashed potatoes behind. She pushes them around aimlessly with her fork.

"Mommy, after we saw the greyhounds, Daddy took me to St. Patrick's Well to get some more holy water."

"Ah, what did ye think of it, James?" Josephine asks.

"It was pretty spectacular. There was something special about it. It just felt...different. It's almost like you could feel the holiness."

Josephine places a giant scoop of potatoes in her mouth and winks at Micheleen.

Micheleen sits up a little straighter. "I didn't know you were into that sort of thing."

"Meesh, there are things about me that you don't know."

James takes a bite of his potatoes. "Auntie Jo, these potatoes are fantastic! What did you do to them?"

"Ah, a bit of this and a bit of that. Boiled potatoes can be somethin' special, can't they?"

Josephine looks over at Micheleen. "Why don't you try them, dearie?"

Micheleen looks down at her plate, over to James, and then over to Josephine. Josephine motions for her to 'just do it.'

Micheleen puts a tiny bit of potatoes on the end of her fork and slowly places it in her mouth. *Woah.*

She goes on to finish every last bite.

After dinner is cleaned up and James leaves, Micheleen looks exhausted and confused.

"Micheleen, why don't ye head to bed. I'll put Maeve to bed again tonight."

"Two days in a row? You're starting to spoil me, Auntie Jo."

Micheleen tells Auntie Jo and Maeve goodnight and heads to her room.

As soon as Josephine is confident Micheleen is asleep, she whispers to Maeve. "Maeve, do ye still have the leprechaun shoes?"

Maeve nods.

"Fetch them and give them to me. Let's tell him yer wish is to get yer hat and video game back. Ye may not need a leprechaun for the important matters in yer life, but ye might as well get yer belongin's back." Josephine smiles.

"Ok, Auntie Jo!"

The pair spend the next few minutes writing the new wish note and placing the shoes outside.

"Now go on to bed, dearie. I'll see ye in the morning."

After Maeve's bedroom lights go out, Josephine sets her alarm for 11:55 p.m.

CHAPTER 32

RUN, MAEVE, RUN

The next morning, Maeve comes running out of her room while Josephine is making breakfast. She sprints down the hall and through the kitchen to where she had left the leprechaun shoes last night. She flings the door open. There upon the stoop is her blue cap and her tablet. On top of them both is a handwritten note in shamrock green ink.

"Auntie Jo! The leprechaun granted my wish!! He returned my stuff!" Maeve squeals with delight.

"That's wonderful, dearie."

Josephine smiles as Maeve places her blue cap back on top of her head.

"Hey, it's too small! That crafty divil changed it to fit his own little head."

Maeve tears it off and fixes the backstrap so it is sized to fit her again. "Much better."

"What does the note say?"

Maeve picks up the note and slowly reads, asking for help on the bigger words:

Yer cap is too big
The tablet, so tirin'
Ye wished for them back
Yet this I'm requirin'
Wear ye blue cap
As much as ye please
But use the screen sparingly
Lest yer brain turn to cheese

"Well, Maeve, what do ye think of that?"

Maeve puts her hands on her hips. "Well, I think he's kind of right about my tablet being boring. God's world is way more fun, especially with you."

Josephine smiles. "Grand! Ye remember that, then, especially when yer a teenager and get yer own *hell phone*."

Maeve giggles. "Okay, Auntie Jo."

Josephine slowly hobbles to the stove to tend to the breakfast she's making. She winces in pain.

"I guess your pain is back today," Maeve pouts.

"'Tis coming back fer sure. But I am so very thankful for that pain-free day yesterday and the time I got to spend with ye."

Maeve runs over and gently hugs Josephine.

"Oh look, yer dah is here to spend the day with ye. Ye better go change yer clothes so that yer ready." Josephine points at the rental car pulling in to the drive.

After Maeve skips off, Josephine walks to the hutch and pulls a green ink pen from her pocket. She rolls it around in her hand as she smiles, then carefully tucks it in one of the drawers.

"Imagination in a child is the doorway to the Divine." She whispers to herself before pushing in the drawer and making her way back to the kitchen.

James parks the car and walks in just as Maeve comes running back out in a striped shirt and jeans.

"Good morning, ladies!"

Maeve dashes over to give him a big hug.

"Mornin', James. I just made eggs and white puddin' for breakfast. Sit down at the table."

"Yes, ma'am."

James takes off his hat and sits as instructed.

"You mean I get to eat vanilla pudding for breakfast?! Mommy never lets me have dessert before lunch." Maeve licks her lips excitedly.

Josephine chuckles. "White puddin' is not like puddin' in America. It's a grain-based sausage."

Maeve scrunches her face in disgust while Josephine serves her a plate. She pokes at the pudding with her fork, letting it roll across her plate.

"So, what do you want to do today, Maeve? We could go into town or you could show me some of the spots you have explored around here?" James asks.

"I want to take you over to the bridge by the river! We can throw rocks and go look for bunnies. We may even get to see a leprechaun!"

James chuckles at Maeve's excitement. "Leprechauns, aye? I can play that game. We've got to make the most of this day since I'm leaving tomorrow."

Maeve stops mid-bite and sets her fork down. "You're leaving tomorrow?"

"Unfortunately, yes. I have to go speak at a medical conference in L.A., and after that I have to go home and go back to work."

James takes a bite of the white pudding and turns to Josephine. "Auntie Jo, this is really good! Much better than I was expecting."

"But Daddy, I don't want you to leave. I want you to stay here with me...and Mommy."

James swallows with a big gulp and wipes his mouth with a napkin. "I'd really like that too, but this is how it has to be now that your mom and I are divorced. Her job is here in Ireland and mine is in the States. I'll come back and visit in a couple months."

"A couple months!? That's way too long!" Maeve pushes herself away from the table, grabs her hat, and sprints out the front door.

James stands and pushes in his chair.

"Thanks for breakfast, Auntie Jo. I better run after her."

Josephine takes a sip of her tea. "Change is hard for everyone, but especially the wee ones."

James grabs his hat and sets out through the front door to track down Maeve while Josephine begins to tidy the kitchen.

Thirty minutes later, James returns looking frazzled. "Auntie Jo, I've looked all over outside your house and by the river bridge. I can't find Maeve anywhere. Do you have any idea where she might have gone?"

"Did ye check the friary?"

"No."

"Let's split up. Ye head to the friary and I'll go to the Holy Spot. We can call each other if we find her."

Josephine grabs her mobile, and, for the first time, she's glad she has it.

"Ok, sounds good. I'll leave a note on the door for Maeve, in case she happens to come back while we are out looking for her."

James writes a note and tapes it to the front door before they set off in opposite directions.

CHAPTER 33

hole in two

Josephine slowly walks the path from her home to the Holy Spot. She's in more pain today, but the motivation to find Maeve pushes her past it.

Josephine crosses paths with Jimmy McCann. "Jimmy, have ye seen my great grand-niece anywhere? I'm afraid she's gotten mad and run off. Her dah and I are tryin' desperately to find her."

Jimmy scratches his chin. "Now that ye mention it, I did see her runnin' up that way towards the Holy Spot about thirty minutes ago. Haven't seen her since."

"Oh, thank God!" Josephine thanks him and continues on her way. She pulls out her cell phone to call James.

"Ole Jimmy McCann said he saw Maeve about thirty minutes ago headin' to the Holy Spot. Meet me up there as quick as ye can."

James sounds relieved and hangs up quickly.

Ahead, Josephine sees the outline of a little girl sitting near the opening of the Fairy Wood. She slowly approaches and lets out a sigh of relief.

"Maeve, thank God I found ye. Ye gave your dah and I such a fright, runnin' off like that."

Maeve sulks as she sits holding her knees to her chest.

"I don't want Daddy to leave. I just want us to be a family again."

Josephine sits down next to Maeve and puts her hand on her knee. "I know, dearie. We just have to keep prayin'. It will happen one day if it's in God's Will, but in the meantime, we must trust Him...even though it's hard."

"Why is it so hard?" Maeve begins to sob.

Josephine just holds her, knowing that no words will make her feel better.

They sit together for a few minutes until Maeve stops crying and her breathing returns to normal.

"Yer dah should be here any minute, should we start walkin' towards where he will be parkin' the car?"

"I guess so."

Maeve stands and kicks the dirt.

"Wait, Auntie Jo. There is something I want to show you first. The leprechaun's hole has gotten huge!"

Maeve runs ahead and beckons for Josephine to follow.

Josephine stands slowly and begins to walk towards Maeve. Maeve stops in front of a big hole in the middle of the field. Her toes creep up to the edge.

"Maeve, back up from there!" Josephine starts walking faster, as fast as her sore bones will allow.

"Look at how big this has gotten! Did the leprechaun do this? Her voice echoes as it bounces out of the deep empty space.

As Josephine reaches an arms-length distance from Maeve, a sensation of impending doom washes over her.

Maeve's toes begin to lean in and she starts to totter as earth begins to crumble along the edge. She flails her arms trying to steady herself.

"Maeve!!!"

Josephine lunges forward and yanks Maeve back with all her might. She clutches Maeve to her chest before she spins back toward the hole as more turf erodes away. They both fall backwards. Maeve lets out a bloodcurdling scream.

CHAPTER 34

THREE AND A THIRD PLAUDITS

Maeve opens her eyes. They feel heavy and everything is blurry. She concedes and lets the weight force them closed.

She's not sure where she is. Surrounded by shades of green, she realizes she must be at the mouth of the enchanted Fairy Wood. A young girl's voice echoes in her ears, "Are ye ready, Maeve?"

Maeve snaps her head to look behind her. It's as if she's looking in a mirror. In front of her stands a little girl, about her own age, with dark hair. Maeve reaches out towards the girl's face, wondering if she's dreaming. "Who- who are you?"

"It's me, Auntie Jo. But you can call me Josie." The little girl smiles. She's missing the same teeth as Auntie Jo, but her mouth matches the youthfulness of her complexion.

"But…What?…How?" Maeve stutters as her skin begins to tingle.

"Aye, now hush." Josie takes her hand and pulls her in.

Suddenly, the dappling daylight that bounces beneath their feet begins to change; colors and vague shapes whirl around them. Miniature people with varying sizes and styles of wings, ears, eyes, and hair form before the two girls. A high-pitched hum morphs into a discernible series of squeals and laughs. Maeve hears them chant, "Joseena, Joseena, Joseena."

"What are they saying?"

"The name they used to call me. Joseena."

A whirl of fairies encircles Josie's head while others hover further above Maeve's. Suddenly, they all freeze. A blast of color and light erupts through the tunnel like a fantastical tidal wave. Calm resumes, but the fairies remain still, as if encased in midair. A larger, more beautiful fairy appears at the top of the branches and descends in front of Josie.

Josie curtsies. "Queen Breena."

Light droplets fall into place as the form of the splendid Fairy Queen materializes before Josie.

"Joseena, we have missed ye. Where is Maeveena?"

"Queen Breena, Maeveena—the Maeveena ye knew as my sister— has passed away."

A loud hush vibrates through the Fairy Wood. The Queen is visibly distraught.

Josie continues, "Don't be sad; she died an old woman who had lived a full life. This here is her very great-granddaughter, named for my dear sister. Queen Breena, I present ye my great-grand niece, Maeve... Maeveena the Younger."

The Queen studies Maeve, floating around her three times in one direction then three the other.

"But how could Maeveena be an old woman while ye, Joseena, are still a girl? Ye and Maeveena were both here just a moon or two ago."

"Queen Breena, we fell into a magical hole that has turned me young again. Maeveena the Younger has been dyin' to see the fairies ever since she got here. I figured now would be a great time to show her around. I hope this is acceptable."

"For ye my dear friend, of course! Queen Breena shouts. "We will have a grand last feast in your honor."

Maeve turns to Josie and whispers, "Why did she say *last* feast?"

"Shhhh. Pay attention," Josie whispers back.

At this, thousands of frozen fairies begin buzzing, humming, and squealing. The excitement in the Fairy Wood is infectious. Maeve's skin begins to tingle once again. The tunnel excels into a spin. Maeve reaches for Josie's hand. The girls' long dark locks blow as they travel through the tunnel of light and sound. As quickly as it began, the spinning stops. Maeve and Josie find themselves seated at a magnificent banquet table with every food imaginable placed in front of them.

The table itself seems big enough to seat a hundred, yet everyone is close enough to speak to each other without effort. The plates at each setting are platinum, ornately inlaid with gold. The silverware is made of rubies and emeralds and the goblets are solid sapphires. The table is a kaleidoscopic array of hues with brightly colored gemstones glistening at every seat.

Maeve is in awe. Josie leans over and whispers directly into Maeve's ear, so as not to be heard by the fairies, "Eat all ye want, but drink not a drop."

Maeve turns and asks, "Why?"

"The fairy meade will put ye in a spell; it'll cause ye to stay here 100 years."

The Queen addresses Maeve. "Did ye ask a question, Maeveena the Younger?"

"No, Queen Breena."

"But I heard ye clearly ask Joseena 'why.' Why what?"

Maeve pauses before regaining her composure. "Josie said not to stare. I asked 'why' and she said it is impolite."

"Maeveena the Younger, I give ye my permission to stare as much as ye wish. Joseena, I see ye still enjoy givin' the orders and squelchin' too much fun."

"Once an older sister, always an older sister, Queen Breena."

The fairy seated next to Queen Breena nods emphatically at this pronouncement. The Queen clears her throat in the direction of the fairy. The nodding pixie looks to the Queen, "Yer pardons, my exalted sister. I was just makin' them feel welcome."

Queen Breena gives a knowing nod to a page standing behind her throne. The page bears an uncanny resemblance to Fergus. The Fergus fairy bangs what looks to be a gong, but it sounds more like thousands of pennies falling in a fine crystal bowl. With this, the Queen makes an announcement.

"As Queen of the Fairies, I welcome back our esteemed, honored, and dear friend, Joseena. I wish to formally introduce to the Circle of the Enchanted, Maeveena the Younger. Three and a third plaudits for Maeveena the Younger!"

A loud chant ensues, "Vim, Vager, Vim, Vager, Vim, Vager Vih!

Josie comments to Maeve, "The most I ever got was two plaudits and a fourth."

The Queen raises her glass, and the rest of the fairies follow. Josie lifts her goblet and Maeve copies her.

"May the feastin' begin!" The Queen drinks from the goblet of sapphire, as do all the other fairies. Josie puts the glass to her lips but without a taste, puts it back down on the table. Maeve does the same before leaning over to Josie.

"Won't they notice we didn't drink any?"

"Now that they've each had a sip, they won't notice a thing, they're all too drunk."

"With just one sip?"

"Fairy Meade, wicked stuff. Now eat up. Ye'll never have food this good again. Until Heaven, of course. Which will be sooner for me than fer ye."

Josie begins sampling the delicacies while Maeve continues to take in the scene. Each fairy is dazzling. Maeve looks to Josie and examines their outfits. "Josie, I think we're underdressed."

"We are, but fairies only really care how they themselves look. They keep the bar low for we mortals. But yer right. We should have worn somethin' more fittin' for this feast. Oh well, have a piece of this!" Josie points to a large bowl.

Maeve digs into the elegant bowl filled with succulent meat. It looks like turkey but is far juicier. It is the most luscious, delicious fowl Maeve has ever had. Rich gravy and buttery mashed potatoes explode in her mouth.

"Josie, there is so much! What meal is this? Breakfast, lunch, what?"

"It's my feast, Maeve, my feast!"

Maeve needs only to imagine her favorite cuisine and it appears before her. Spaghetti and meatballs, fried chicken, pepperoni pizza, chocolate cake, and cotton candy are invoked with a simple thought. They sample every item on the table, each one better than the last. Josie blinks and a moment later two delectable chocolate éclairs materialize.

Josie looks at Maeve. "We need to go now!"

"Now? But what about the éclairs?"

"There is no time! We must go now!" Josie shouts with urgency.

Maeve is startled, but she stands to follow Josie, who leads her down a long, colorful, baroque style hallway.

At the end of the hall, Josie studies a series of three doors. "Let me see, which one is it?"

The paneling and decoration on each are elaborately carved in intricate Celtic knots and lines. At first glance, the doors seem nearly identical. Maeve is curious as to where each leads.

"What's the difference? They are all right next to each other. They can't open to places very far away."

"One is a door to mortality."

"Where's that?"

"That's death."

"Oh. What about the other two?"

"Another leads to the banquet hall we just came from. But if we go through that door, it's worse than drinkin' a vat of that meade. We'll be here fer a thousand years at least. One door will take us back to the present time."

"How can you tell which to pick?"

"The answer is in the carvin's. One has a skull for death, one has a goblet for the fairy realm, and the third has a shamrock for Ireland. Here goes!"

Josie takes Maeve's hand and opens the door to the far

right. Upon turning the knob, the door flings open and the two are sucked through the opening. They whoosh along a long tube, landing with a thud on their backsides just outside the opposite end of the Fairy Wood that they had entered only minutes ago.

CHAPTER 35

SOMETHING NOT RIGHT

Micheleen's cell phone begins vibrating on her hip. She had just sat down in the conference room to a dozen unhappy looks from her peers, scolding her for missing so much of the day for personal business.

Micheleen looks at the caller ID: it's James, he can wait. She lets it vibrate. After a few minutes more, the vibrating starts again. *What is he thinking? He knows better than to pester me at work. Why does he always have to be so persistent?*

When he calls a third time, Micheleen reaches down and shuts the phone off.

She sits there listening to the monotonous ramblings of the HR Director, wondering what Maeve and Auntie Jo are doing. Suddenly, a sense of dread overtakes her. She dials her voicemail.

James voice on the recording says, "Meesh, answer your

phone! Something has happened to Maeve and Auntie Jo. Call me!"

"Oh no!" Micheleen yells as her stomach lurches. She jumps up and rushes out of the meeting, leaving behind a room full of aggravated executives.

Sprinting to her car, Micheleen punches the redial on her cell phone.

James answers, "Meesh? Finally!"

"James, what's going on?!"

"They fell in a hole. Meet me at the hospital now!" James hangs up.

Micheleen flings her phone on the passenger seat and drives off, a sickening feeling growing in her stomach. She's never heard that tone in James' voice before. He never panics.

Micheleen's heart is in her throat.

A hole!? What in the world?! How is Maeve, my baby? Why wasn't I there?! I should have been there with her! Maybe I could have stopped this from happening. Please, God, let Maeve and Auntie Jo be okay.

Suddenly, work and her career ambitions seem unimportant, just a path that has taken away precious time with her daughter.

Micheleen screeches to a halt outside the hospital, pulling off the street and leaving her car parked diagonally in a parallel space. She rushes in and is escorted to a waiting room where she finds James pacing back and forth.

"James! What happened?!"

"Auntie Jo and Maeve fell in a sinkhole..."

"A sinkhole!? But how?..."

"It was up near the Holy Spot. Authorities think it must have opened up during all the rain yesterday."

"What were they doing at the Holy Spot without you? I thought you were going to be spending the day with Maeve?"

James runs his fingers through his hair. "I was. Maeve got mad when I told her I was leaving tomorrow. She ran off during breakfast and I couldn't find her, so Auntie Jo and I split up looking. Jimmy McCann saw Auntie Jo try to save Maeve from falling in the hole. He said they both lost their balance. Auntie Jo broke Maeve's fall and likely saved her life. Maeve is in surgery for a broken arm, but she's going to be fine. Auntie Jo might not make it. She's still unconscious and in critical condition. A twelve-foot fall isn't good for anyone, but especially someone her age."

The doors to the waiting room swing open and Father Adrian rushes in, not noticing Micheleen and James. He stops at the desk.

"I was called to give Last Rites to Josephine Byrne."

The nurse quickly leads Father Adrian through a double set of doors.

"James, did you hear that?! He said Last Rites!" Micheleen begins to sob.

James pulls her close and embraces her.

After a few moments, Micheleen's breathing returns to a normal pace in James' arms.

"Hey, do you want to go to the chapel? I noticed there is one right down the hall. Maeve will be in surgery for at least another thirty minutes. I'll give the nurse my cell number and she can call as soon as we're able to see either one of them."

Micheleen's voice catches in her throat. The words don't seem to match the mouth they are coming from. "Yeah...I'd like that."

They walk down the sterile hall and through a wooden door marked "Chapel."

The room is sparsely decorated. It contains a few rows of simple pews and one large crucifix.

Micheleen and James walk to the front and sit in the first-row pew. Micheleen reaches for James' hand. He squeezes it tightly.

"C'mon Meesh. Let's pray."

Micheleen kneels next to her ex-husband. In this moment, she can't remember doubting her love for him.

They bow their heads.

"Dear Heavenly Father, I'm a little rusty at this, so bear with me. Please let Maeve and Auntie Jo recover. Protect them and heal them. Wash away our fears and fill our hearts with faith and hope. Let the love and support Meesh and I have for each other, through Your will, strengthen us to get through this and all other difficult times. Amen."

The flood gates open and tears stream down Micheleen's face. She and James look at each other and embrace with the total power they each possess.

CHAPTER 36

pretty in pink

Maeve tries to open her eyes again but can't. She hears metal clinking and a rumbling of voices in the background.

"She needs more. Turn up the drip."

A few seconds later, Maeve is back in her room at Auntie Jo's house.

"Oh good, yer back!" Josie smiles. "Let's change into some of yer fancy party dresses that yer mam made ye! I must look nice for this occasion."

Maeve wonders to what occasion Josie is referring. Meanwhile, Josie runs her fingers over a series of elaborate dresses hanging in the closet.

"This pink one is brilliant!" Josie admires the stitching and embroidery before trying it on.

"I've never worn somethin' so beautiful in my entire life!"

Maeve looks at herself in the mirror. Somehow, she is already wearing her own pink party dress.

Josie and Maeve admire their matching looks in the mirror.

"Yer Granny and I would have killed fer gowns like these. I look as fancy as Queen Breena herself, don't I?"

"Pink looks amazing on you!"

Josie spins in the mirror. "I think yer right, Maeve! And all these years I've thought blue was my color."

Maeve thinks about all the colors painted on Auntie Jo's walls. "I think you need some pink in your house."

Josie taps her finger to her chin. "Ye may be right about that. Pink is the color of rejoicing and today is surely full of that!"

Josie takes one more turn in the mirror, "Do ye want to go back to the fairy party now that we'd be properly dressed?"

"Yes! I'm drooling thinking about all that yummy food."

"Come on, let's go!"

Josie grabs Maeve's wrist and the pair walk outside and over to the old castle gate. They glide through the ancient timbers like wind through the gaps. Once over the threshold of the castle keep, they are transported back to the fairy feast, where hardly anything has changed since they left.

Queen Breena remains seated on her throne, Fergus fairy flies in the same spot where they left him, and the food they had sampled lies on their plates waiting to be finished. And there, off to the side are the luscious éclairs they abandoned, untouched.

Josie picks up the shining plate and takes a bite. "Wow, these are delicious!" She holds her éclair up to the sky and says, "Maeve, eat these in remembrance of me."

Maeve giggles, but Josie makes strong eye contact.

"I'm serious, Maeve. I want ye to promise that every time ye eat a chocolate éclair, ye will think of yer dear Auntie Jo up in

Heaven. Let it remind ye that Jesus, Mary, Joseph, and I want ye to join us one day. So ye must follow Jesus throughout yer life – He is the only way to the Father."

"Ok, Josie. I pinkie promise."

Maeve extends her little finger towards Josie and they shake on it.

Maeve takes a bite of her éclair. It's an explosion of buttery light layers of pastry filled with velvety, creamy, delightfully sweet custard, and topped with a decadent rich chocolate icing.

Josie reaches for her and Maeve's goblets, dumping the meade into the goblet of the fairy sitting next to them. Josie takes a bottle of holy water from her pocket and refills the goblets with the safe liquid.

"Cheers, Maeve!"

"Cheers, Josie!"

The girls clink and drink.

CHAPTER 37

Baggage Unpacked

James and Micheleen walk into Josephine's hospital room. She is lying in the bed, attached to numerous machines making all sorts of noise.

"She is not responsive right now, but she can still hear ye. I will give ye some time with her alone." The nurse draws the curtain closed around them and walks out of the room.

Micheleen walks over and sits in a chair by Josephine's head.

"Auntie Jo, I won't ever be able to thank you enough. You saved Maeve's life. If you hadn't broken her fall..." Micheleen begins to sob, unable to finish her sentence.

James puts his hand on her shoulder and tries to fill in where she left off.

"Thank you, Auntie Jo. We are forever grateful for you."

A tear falls down James' cheek as they both stand frozen in time, trying to make sense of what is unfolding in front of them.

James crouches down so he's eye-to-eye with Micheleen. "Meesh, there is something I need to say."

Micheleen wipes her tears with her sleeve and looks at James.

"The last time we sat next to someone who was dying, I made a big mistake."

Micheleen sniffs and scrunches her nose. "What do you mean?"

James grabs Micheleen's hand. "I mean, I should have let you grieve for your father in whatever way you saw fit. I should have let you say and do whatever made you feel better, without judgement. I should have let you pray. A husband should make his wife's load easier to carry, not put his own baggage on her."

"Your baggage? What are you talking about?"

James clears his throat. "When my grandmother died, there was a horrible priest who made me never want to step foot in a church again. When I saw you praying next to your dad's bed, it brought all those hard memories back, and I took that out on you. I'm sorry. I'm so, so sorry. Being here, seeing Maeve pray, stepping foot in church again, made me realize how wrong I was."

James' eyes soften as he implores, "Can you find it in your heart to forgive me?"

Micheleen flings herself into James' arms with a force that takes James by surprise.

"I guess that's a 'yes.'" James chuckles with thanks.

Just then, Josephine raises her arm and starts trying to remove her oxygen mask.

"James! She's moving!"

James jumps up and helps Josephine move her mask to the side. "What is it, Auntie Jo? What do you need?"

Josephine tries to speak, but her voice is scratchy and breathless.

"James, I can't understand her. What is she trying to say?"

"Pocket!" Josephine screeches out. "Give…to…Maeve."

"I think she's trying to tell us there is something in her pocket she wants us to give to Maeve," James says.

Josephine nods her head before resting it on her pillow peacefully. The monitor gives a long, extended beep.

CHAPTER 38

TIME TO GO

Josie weaves through the drunken fairies, reaching Maeve on the dance floor. "Maeve, it's time for ye to go."

Maeve keeps dancing and laughing. "But I'm having so much fun with the fairies."

Josie reaches out to try to grab Maeve's arm and Maeve pushes her away, accidentally knocking over a goblet of fairy meade. As the blue goblet shatters, the music stops, the dancing halts, and all eyes fall upon the splattered potion. Queen Breena rises from her royal seat.

"Maeveena the Younger, this must be cleaned up immediately!"

Maeve grabs a spun silk napkin and kneels down to the spill. Queen Breena holds up her scepter.

"Halt! Maeveena the Younger, I realize ye are unfamiliar with the laws of our realm. I shall educate ye. Anyone who drips, drops, slops, or squabs the royal meade must personally slop every dropped drop."

Maeve stands there stunned, unsure of what to do.

Josie jumps in. "Queen Breena, I know it is not yer custom, but since the feast is in my honor, would ye make an exception and allow me to clean up the meade for her?"

Queen Breena flutters her wings and places her finger on her cheek. "Hmm. I suppose since the party is for ye, I could allow an exception, just this once."

"Thank ye, Queen Breena. Is it okay if I dare to ask for one more favor?"

"Go on…"

"Maeveena the Younger must be getting back now. May I walk her to the door?"

Queen Breena pouts. "But the party has just started. She can't leave yet."

Josie gets closer to Queen Breena and looks her in the eyes. "She truly must leave this instant. She is being called back to her parents by the Lord. Ye must allow her to leave. I will personally lick up every drop of meade and will stay with ye for as long as the good Lord allows."

Queen Breena extends her hand so the two can shake on it. "Alright, go on then. Walk with Maeveena the Younger to the door."

The fairies watch in silence as Josie escorts Maeve to the three doors.

Maeve whispers. "No! I'm not leaving here without you."

Josie whispers back. "Ye must. Ye have no choice in the matter."

"But I'm the one who spilled the meade! I should be the one to clean it up and to have to stay here."

As they approach the doors, Josie puts her hands on Maeve's shoulders.

"I'm putting myself in yer place, so that ye can go on to live a full life. I've spent enough time on Earth and now our Heavenly Father is calling me home. But ye...ye still have a callin' to complete."

Maeve starts to tear up. "I...I...I can't go without you. I'm going to miss you too much." A warm tear falls down her face and lands on her chest, leaving a darkened circle on the pink satin.

"I'm going to miss ye too, but one day, God willing, we can be together again. Today may be one full of sorrow, but because of Jesus' sacrifice, joy follows. Do ye understand what I'm saying?"

"I think so." Maeve spits out through the tears.

"Hurry up, Joseena! We are all waiting for ye." Queen Breena yells from a distance.

"I'll be there in a minute, Queen Breena," Josie hollers over her shoulder before turning back to Maeve.

"A wise man once told me these words, and I'm going to repeat them to ye."

Josie grabs Maeve by the shoulders.

"Yer faith is yer lifeline. Cling to it and to yer Mother. Ye must trust the Lord yer God with all of yer heart, soul, and mind, even when it's painful....just like Our Lady did."

Josie looks back to Queen Breena and holds up her index finger, then turns back to Maeve.

"Today and in the days to come, ye may feel sorrow. But when ye do, think about our Blessed Mother on Good Friday, the day of Jesus' torture and death. She must have been as sorrowful as a human can be. But then, after the darkness of death, think of the joy she must have experienced when she saw her Resurrected Son for the first time. Imagine that meeting!"

Maeve stops crying and bites her lips.

"Okay, I will try…and Josie…one more thing. I'm sorry for knocking over that meade. It's my fault that you are being punished."

"Don't worry, dearie. 'Tis all part of God's plan. Now give me a hug. Ye must be gettin' on yer way."

Maeve leaps into Josie's arms as they bear hug.

After a few moments, Josie peels Maeve's hands off of her.

"Go on now, Maeve. Be brave. Be strong. Stay close to Jesus through his Mother. She will take care of ye. Now, don't delay. Go through that door." Josie points to the one that will take her back to Ireland.

Maeve grabs the knob and blows Josie a final kiss before walking through the door.

CHAPTER 39

Medal Mettle

Maeve opens her eyes and sees the faces of her mom and dad leaning over her.

"Wha- Where am I?"

"Sweetie, you've had quite the fall. You broke your arm and had to have emergency surgery to fix it."

Maeve looks down at her arm and sees a pink cast, the same shade as the dresses she and Josie had been wearing just a few moments ago. She looks around the room, trying to remember something.

"Do you remember anything about what happened?" James asks.

Maeve puts her hand to her head and closes her eyes. "I remember running towards the Holy Spot, but I don't remember anything else except for Auntie Jo being a kid...and Queen Breena...and the fairies...and Josie making me come back...and..."

"Whoa, whoa, honey." James chuckles, "Slow down. You hit

your head when you fell and also have a slight concussion. It may take a while for your memory to come back. They also have you on some pain killers, which have some interesting side effects...like fairy encounters." He strokes her hair and smiles.

Her mom is smiling too, but there is a look of sadness behind her eyes.

"Mommy, are you sad because Auntie Jo died?"

Micheleen's eyes grow wide, "Maeve, how did you kn–"

"Don't worry, Mommy. She's with Jesus now."

A slight grin crosses Maeve's face. "And because she shared Jesus with us, we can be with Him one day too."

Micheleen's eyes tear up again and the three share a long overdue family hug.

"Maeve, there is something that Auntie Jo wanted you to have. It was in her pocket during the accident."

Micheleen extends her arm and drops the blue rosary and a cool silver medallion in her hand.

Maeve looks at the medal and sees a picture of the Blessed Mother with the words *Our Lady of Sorrows* written underneath.

Maeve smiles. "Josie told me that I need to stay close to the Blessed Mother, that she would understand my sorrow and help me grow closer to Jesus."

"Sweetie, who is Josie?" Micheleen asks.

"Auntie Jo, as a little girl. She saved me from being stuck with the fairies forever." Maeve holds the rosary out to her father. "Here, Daddy, Auntie Jo actually wants you to have this."

James takes the rosary with a sense of awe.

Micheleen and James look at each other and smile. Micheleen suggests, "Maeve, get some rest now."

Maeve sits back and closes her eyes.

CHAPTER 40

Sacrificial Love

Maeve, Micheleen, and James sit solemnly in the front pew as Father Adrian proceeds with the Funeral Mass. He approaches the podium. The church is filled beyond capacity with mourners.

Father Adrian looks out over the packed church and reminds himself that Josephine more than deserved every mourner present, along with every prayer said in her name. He thinks about the Cambrai homily, the oldest known Irish homily in existence, and marvels about how Josephine in some way touched each of the three types of martyrdom discussed in it.

He pictures Josephine's signature hat. Was it a coincidence that blue martyrdom is suffering, penance, and cleansing – and she happened to wear a blue hat during all those years of trials?

Father Adrian recalls delivering the sopping wet hat to the white-haired woman sitting upon the high stool. Was it a mere coincidence that shortly after her American relatives turned up, she lost her hat and donned her hair? White martyrdom is when someone parts, for the sake of God, from their plans – exactly what Josephine did by taking in her extended family.

He thinks about red martyrdom, the martyrdom of enduring a cross or destruction for the sake of Christ. Josephine died in an act of sacrifice, helping her loved ones to grow closer to Jesus.

He gazes back down at the empty podium in front of him, saying a quick prayer and asking the Holy Spirit to speak through him. Though he had labored and toiled trying to pen a proper eulogy for Josephine, no suitable words would present themselves. Putting his full trust in the Father, the Son, and the Holy Ghost, Father Adrian resigns himself to winging it. He clears his mind as he clears his throat.

"I stand here in front of all of ye today to celebrate the life, and bear witness to the passin', of our beloved sister, Josephine.

"I will confess, fer years I'd been silently at odds with her practice of piseoga, but as a priest and a son of people who respected the old ways, I tended on most accounts to look the other way, prayin' her heart would be judged by its intent and not her practice.

"I was always happy to see her and her floppy blue hat in daily Mass, but I didn't ponder her much beyond that. I ask ye, what could an aging, funny-hat-wearing woman of superstition teach me, a learned Holy man?

"This frail woman, racked with arthritis from head to toe, a healer of supposedly all but herself, could barely lift her own self up from genuflectin'. From worldly appearances, she was a soul spent, just markin' time until she could go to her eternal rest, all the productive days of her life well behind her.

"But, as God often does, He had other ideas – to use this woman, not in the form of Josephine the daily Mass attendee, but as Auntie Jo, a courageous, mighty servant of the Lord.

"What is the difference between Josephine and Auntie Jo ye may ask? Nothing and everything. Like the Holy Trinity, this ordinary woman was known by different names for different callings in her life. To some of ye she was Josie Maxey, a girl ye grew up with. Others of ye met her as Josephine Byrne, a healer with knowledge of cures that only our ancestors could know. Others still, knew her by a third name: Auntie Jo."

Father Adrian looks down at little Maeve. Maeve smiles, her grin re-routing the track of gentle tears that grace her apple cheeks.

"Each of her callings and names were valuable. However, her vocation as Auntie Jo durin' her final few days of service to God was perhaps the most inspirin' event I will ever witness on this earth.

"As Josephine, she was a faithful parishioner who had fallen victim to the mortal condition known as age. As Auntie Jo, her physical frailties melted away, allowin' her to lift yours truly, all twelve stone of me, up to the Creator Himself, finally bringin' my heart to its sacred purpose."

The priest grabs the sides of the pulpit.

"The sound of this may cause ye to question my mental faculties, but, as God is my witness, 'tis true. She and I shared a day of…well…we had a miraculous swap of sorts. For the first time in my life, I was forced to experience sincere empathy. I was able to look into Josephine's soul, to see every affliction she possessed, physically and spiritually. This experience made me extend beyond myself and experience her existence, to take on her doubts and live her pain the way a true servant of God's people must.

"Through this sacred swap of ours, Josephine proceeded to do the work of Christ. In her last few days, Auntie Jo accomplished what even an army of angels could not. She passed on a priceless gift, a sacred gift, a gift rarely offered: the gift of sacrifice. She sacrificed her time to breathe faith into her family, and she sacrificed herself to save another.

"Josephine bestowed on me and others here the testimony that not only allows a soul to be willin' to die for Christ, but also enlightens the soul to make the ultimate sacrifice, the hardest act of all: the commitment to LIVE for Christ. Josephine did this. Auntie Jo did this. Auntie Jo does this still. For she is alive in Heaven. I pray this very moment she stands before the Face of God, her new heart overflowing, surrounded by the angels, saints, and her loved ones gone before her. She is gone from us for now, taking a bit of our own hearts with her to heaven while at the same time continuing to live in what remains of our earthly hearts, telling us to 'be healed and go to Confession.' Am I right?"

A chorus of agreement rumbles across the heads in the pews.

Father Adrian concludes, "May we all keep Auntie Jo in our hearts and use her example to guide us for the rest of our mortal days. May God Bless us, and may God Bless our Josephine... our dear Auntie Jo. In the name of the Father and of the Son and of the Holy Ghost. Amen."

CHAPTER 41

Going Home

With the conclusion of the Funeral Mass, people spill from the Friary and out into the street. Micheleen, Maeve, and James take their place at the head of the Funeral March behind the shiny black hearse. The pitch-colored crowd winds their way on foot through the town and up Waterford Road to Josephine's final resting place.

There, between the headstone of her faithful husband, Teddy, and her sister, Maeve, is a freshly dug hole waiting for the small wood casket to be lowered. The mourners look on while tears, sobs, and many a Sign of the Cross are made.

Maeve takes everything in as Auntie Jo's casket is lowered in the ground. She walks over to Father Adrian and hands him her bottle of Patrick's Well water. Father Adrian uncaps the small glass vessel and sprinkles the drops over the plain wooden box.

Maeve looks up to gaze upon a marble angel planted across the path of the graveyard. Silently, the great white owl perches on the angel's shoulder, bearing witness to his friend's final bow. The white owl takes flight as the sun breaks through and shines upon Maeve.

Father Adrian concludes the Funeral rite. "May Josephine's soul eternally rest in peace. Amen."

James puts his arm around Micheleen. Micheleen looks to him. "Thank you for being here for all of this...for Maeve...and for me."

"I'll be here for you forever, Meesh...if you'll let me."

Micheleen looks into James' eyes. "I won't just let you be, James...I *want* you to be."

Maeve grabs her mother's hand. "Mommy, after we go back to Castlecottage today, can we go home? I mean, really home... to America?"

Micheleen looks at Maeve and then to James. "Yes, Maeve. Yes, we can."

"Yay!" Maeve jumps up and down. "Can we stop and get some chocolate éclairs at Kehoe's, in Auntie Jo's honor?

CHAPTER 42

A New Door to Open

Maeve sits next to her dad in the rear of Fergus' car, savoring a chocolate éclair and thinking about Auntie Jo being with Jesus.

Micheleen and Fergus are in front as Fergus speeds along the road, turning on to the long drive leading up to Castlecottage. As the car passes all the trees and the cottage comes into view, Maeve's eyes widen and her jaw drops.

"Look at the door! It's pink!"

Micheleen turns to Fergus. "Fergus, did you paint Auntie Jo's front door?"

"No ma'am. The door was brown as a hare when I left it but a few hours ago."

After Fergus parks the car, everyone gets out and walks up to the pink door. James reaches out to touch it.

"It's dry."

Fergus touches it too. "Set as if painted a week ago."

The three adults look on in disbelief. Maeve looks to Heaven with a chocolate smile, feeling the embrace of Auntie Jo in her heart.

"I love you, Auntie Jo!"

MATER MEDIA

TO MAKE **Jesus Christ** **MORE KNOWN** AND **MORE LOVED** BY **MORE PEOPLE**

THROUGH MEDIA

Discover uniquely inspiring BOOKS, soul stirring FILM projects and the CELEBRATE CATHOLIC MARRIAGE EXPERIENCE at MaterMedia.org

Made in the USA
Columbia, SC
13 January 2025